For J.

Train Flight

The Sanctuary

ELIZABETH NEWTON

Order this book online at www.trafford.com
or email orders@trafford.com

Most Trafford titles are also available at major online book retailers.

All scriptures are taken from the Holy Bible.

Printed in the United States of America.

ISBN: 978-1-4669-4006-2 (sc)
ISBN: 978-1-4669-4005-5 (e)

Trafford rev. 01/10/2013

 www.trafford.com

North America & international
toll-free: 1 888 232 4444 (USA & Canada)
phone: 250 383 6864 ♦ fax: 812 355 4082

Note:

This story is the third of the Train Flight series. It can be read by itself, but it is also part of the ongoing adventures of Evie and Paulo in the Train with the Captain.

Others in the series so far:

Moon Man
The Birth Of Salvation

Contents

Chapter One

The Consultant

"Next patient please," said a tall, young woman emerging stiffly from a dimly lit consulting room. Glasses, modest white blouse, black pencil skirt, hair in a loose bun.

Another woman, awkward and unsure of herself, stood up from a chair in the waiting room and followed the consultant into the room. When the consultant sat down behind her desk, she could hear her boss' words in her head: "Remember, it is important not to refer to them as patients. They are clients. *Clients.*"

"Why don't you tell me what's on your mind?" she said after settling the visitor into a comfy chair.

"Well I, suppose I'm just so stressed at the moment, what with work—the extra hours they've given me. My husband isn't able to get any time off work at the moment so he's not able to stay home with the children. I would normally of course but we need the second income because of all the fees and bills and tax and just . . . everything! Cindy, my youngest has just had some tests done and we've been told that she should go to a special school, which means higher fees and costs for equipment and learning materials and private tutoring. Max wants to start learning the guitar and I haven't the heart to say no.

1

I always wanted my children to be musical. And Caleb, my eldest is supposed to be going on this trip with his football team up to the Gold Coast—I just don't know how I'm supposed to cope. We're running out of money fast!"

The consultant was nodding sympathetically.

"George—that's my husband—is trying to get a pay rise, but I don't think that's going to happen any time soon. You see, I need the extra hours at work to pay for everything, but it only means I'm going to have to get a baby sitter in for the evenings after school, which means *more* money." She sighed a big, stressed, sigh.

The consultant nodded again and spoke in a calm, breathy voice. "Yes. I understand your predicament." She got up and walked around to the front of her desk. "It is very *stressful* isn't it?" She looked at her client with kind, caring eyes. Her voice was smooth and velvety—like she was trying to calm a spooked horse. She put her hand up to her glasses and slowly slipped them off the end of her nose.

The worried woman continued. "Sometimes I wish it could all just go away. For all of it to just sort itself out without me having to do *anything*."

"Or even . . . escape it all. Get away."

"Oh if only it could be that simple. If only there was a quick solution like that. But I know that's not possible. I just came here so that I could have a good chat about it. Today's my one day off for quite a while."

"Let your stress go, right now in this room."

The woman let out a big breath of air and closed her eyes.

"Imagine, you're free. You have no responsibilities. No one is relying on you. You have nothing to do. You don't need to feed anyone. You don't need to drive the car anywhere. In fact, you have no car . . . you don't need one."

The woman sighed again and smiled. "Oh, that sounds good. Problem is, all my problems are back as soon as I jump back in the car."

"You have no car. Remember?" The consultant smiled and looked to the floor for a second. Then she said in her soft and gentle voice, "Come through."

The woman opened her eyes and looked up. "Through to where?"

The consultant was indicating an adjoining room with her outstretched arm and a kind, welcoming smile. "Another consulting room it's, more private."

Odd, thought the woman, but she wandered through all the same.

Once the client had walked through the inner door, the calm, sympathetic consultant stepped in with her and quietly closed the door behind her.

And that's when the blinding light and the terrible screeching started. That's the moment when Linda Patterson's life slipped through her fingers like sand.

*   *   *

The Captain and Paulo were standing around on a grassy hill top, gazing around at the beautiful vast expanse of countryside. All there was, as far as the eye could see was bright, lush green grass, blue sky . . . and nature. Just nature. The smell of nature, the sound of nature, a perfect picture of clean, refreshing nature.

Evie Bamford was soaking it all up, wandering off and enjoying the sunshine.* She seemed unaffected by the fact that the three travellers had no idea where they were. That something had gone wrong with the controls of the Train.♦

"So if we're not on your planet Captain," said Paulo, "where are we exactly?"

"Well I hate to fill you with anxious doubt and insecurity," replied the Captain, "but I have absolutely no idea. I mean, usually when I land on a strange planet, I could give you a rough idea of at least what galaxy we're in. But I regret to say, I can't for the moment. We were meant to have landed on my home planet but . . . this is nothing like my home."

"This place is beautiful though."

"Exactly. Definitely can't be my home."

"But this kind of landscape . . ." began Paulo, "well it could very well be Serothia."*

"It could very well be Evie's Earth too. It could very well be any number of different planets. That's why it's so hard to say where it is we are."

---

*   Evie Bamford was from Earth like you and me, (I assume), and more specifically, from Adelaide, Australia. She was fourteen and her bursting curiosity was what had thrown her and the Captain together.

♦   **Train** /treɪn/, *n.* [1] a set of carriages or wagons, whether self propelled or connected to a locomotive. [2] to discipline and instruct a person or animal to perform specified actions. [3] a vehicle made from the wreckage of a railway steam train specially built to travel in space and time, the paint work of which enabling it to 'appear' invisible.

*   Serothia is Paulo's home planet. It is found in the Black Eye galaxy (or M64) and it's a place where everyone is always really nice to each other.

"I see what you mean. So what do you reckon? Those three days Mallory was stuck inside the Train, he battered up the controls a bit?"

"In a fit of rage probably, trying to get free." *

"What do we do then, look for him or what?"

"No, since he's decided to run off—never to be seen again, he's no longer our problem. He'll be stuck here. Come on, let's get back inside the Train and see if we can get it back on track. It's time I got Evelyn home." On his way to the Train door, he called out, "Evelyn, come on, let's go!"

There was no reply.

"Evie?" called Paulo.

They looked at each other and the Captain stepped down from the Train to look around.

"You don't think Mallory . . ."

"No, look," said the Captain, relieved but slightly perplexed. "There she is."

"What's she doing?"

Evie was walking down the hill, taking slow, even steps. In between her hands in front of her chest, she was holding a white flower that she'd picked from the ground.

It's so beautiful here, she was thinking. *I think I want to stay here forever. So peaceful. Quiet. Tranquil. Peaceful. What's that beautiful sound? I want to be near it.*

"Evelyn!" the Captain called, cupping his hands to his mouth.

---

* Mallory was a man they had recently met who wanted to steal the Train to escape and travel around the universe by himself, probably only to do evil deeds and plan devious schemes for his own benefit. The Captain had been on his way to returning him back home and now here they were.

There was no way she could have not heard him. But she kept on walking, like she was in some kind of trance.

"I'll go get her," said Paulo and took off with a jog down the hill.

Not long after that, the Captain stopped him abruptly and yelled, "No, stop Paulo! Get away!"

Paulo's eyes widened with terrified alarm. They were both looking at a strange sort of glow, pulsating all around Evie's body. With every second, it was getting larger and larger and then there was an ear-piercing screeching sound.

What a perfect place. The air is so fresh. The ground is so soft. I want to live here. I want to touch that sound. I want to drink it!

Both the Captain and Paulo were covering their ears. The light around Evie was almost blinding them, and so they had to cover their eyes too.

But Evie was captivated. *How can a place be so lovely? I love it. I love it. I want to get closer. Closer. I want to dance. I want to bathe in this place. Let me closer. Closer!*

The sound stopped. Paulo and the Captain, cowering on the ground and shielding their eyes and ears, slowly looked up. The light, the sound, everything was gone. Including Evelyn. All that remained was the beautiful blissful landscape.

"Where did she go?"

The Captain got up onto his feet, frowning worriedly. He looked all around them. The Train was still there,[*]

---

[*] He could see it when he put on his brown leather driving goggles or slid on a pair of special glasses.

but this beautiful, calm, peaceful place now had an eerie, disturbing silence about it. There was one thing terribly wrong with it. It seemed to have just swallowed up Evelyn!

Chapter Two

The Butterfly Net

For a few seconds, Evie found that she couldn't open her eyes. They felt glued together with sleep, the stuff that's delivered by the Sand Man throughout the night.

When she *did* get them open, all she could see was a high ceiling. She blinked a few times to get her vision into focus, and staring down at her was a white, buzzing florescent light. She felt woozy, but tried to sit up anyhow to take in the rest of her surroundings. She could now see that she was in a white hospital bed, with white sheets and a white blanket.

She looked around the eerily silent room. It was large and her bed wasn't the only one. Eight or nine other beds were lined up along the walls, parallel with each other. Only, they were empty beds. Hers was the only one occupied at present.

The walls were wood-paneled half way up and then above that, painted white. There were square windows spread evenly along one wall, but all the curtains were closed across them. They were thick canvas yellow and orange curtains, as if someone had tried to brighten up the room with them—and failed.

When she saw that there were other sections of the room that she couldn't see due to its apparent T-shape, Evie lifted the bed covers off of her and swung her legs around to sit up on the side of the bed. In doing so, she discovered that her clothes were white as well. Gone were her jeans, pink T-shirt and favourite hooded jacket. All that remained was a white nighty, over the top of her knee-high black and white striped socks. *

She couldn't understand it. One minute, she was with the Captain and Paulo on this beautiful lush green stretch of land and the next, she was here.

"This isn't the right place," the Captain had said.

"Of *course* it's the right place," Evie had replied. "It's *perfect!*"

. . . And that's the last thing she remembered.

She stood up slowly from the bed and looked around cautiously. No one seemed to be about. As she walked forward, more parts of the room were revealed to her—but it was all much the same. It looked like an old 1940s hospital or something. *Perhaps I'm in the 40s*, she thought. Now that she'd met the Captain—anything was possible.

She reached the middle of the room. Either side of her were the rows of beds, which made it kind of an isle. The empty beds freaked her out. She couldn't stop looking at them to double check that they really were *all* empty. It looked as though they had never been slept in. *Maybe it's an abandoned 40s hospital . . .*

"Up and about I see?"

---

* She panicked all of a sudden, and checked quickly for her underwear–thankfully they were still there too.

The voice made Evie jump out of her skin. It came from behind her, and when she looked, alarmed and unnerved, she saw a young woman in a white nurse's outfit. She was utterly plain looking. There was nothing about her that stood out as a distinguishable feature.

Evie just had to ask the inevitable question. She did it very politely. "W-where am I, please?"

"In the Infirmary."

"What's an infirmary?"

The nurse looked as though she couldn't understand someone not understanding the term 'infirmary'. "The rest bay . . . the hospice."

"As in, hospital?"

Another polite smile. "The word 'hospital' has so much stigma attached to it, we feel."

"What's stigma?"

"I think you ought to be getting back to bed, D14. You may need some more rest before we release you. It is important you understand that there's no hurry to recover. You take your time."

The nurse tried to hustle her back into bed, but Evie protested.

"Recover from what, and . . . what did you call me?"

"In you get, there's a good girl."

Evie stood her ground. "I feel fine! I don't need any more rest! Tell me where I am, please."

"I told you. The Infirmary."

"But *where*. The Infirmary of *where*?"

"Surely you know where you are. You're in the Sanctuary, my dear."

Evie frowned, confused. She was getting quite nervous with the nurse's calmness and genteel manner.

"Alright, sister. It's alright, I'll deal with this one." A new voice was in the room. Evie looked to the door and there stood another woman in a nurse's uniform. This one was older and matronly. She didn't look as civil as the younger nurse—who now gave the older one a little nod and walked out of the room.

The matron spoke to Evie with a husky, insensitive voice. "You'll have to excuse 81Z3, she doesn't realise you're new here."

"Did you say *eighty-one zed three?*"

"Yes. My colleague." Then she said in a new breath. "Now that you're out of bed and feeling up to things, you'd better follow me. To the Recovery Room." She started walking, expecting Evelyn to follow her.

Well, the woman was her only hope of answers, so she did follow. "Look, what's going on? What is this place?"

Without stopping to look back, the matron replied, "Everything will be explained to you presently. Just follow me for the time being."

Paulo slowly got up off the ground, looking all around him at the wide open country side. "What happened?" he asked the Captain.

The Captain returned his glasses to one of his pockets and then scratched his head. "Transmat beam, teleportation, hole in the ground . . . could be any number of things."

"But can I just check with you—that I'm not seeing things. She has actually *completely vanished* hasn't she?"

"Well, we can't be too sure of that either. She could be there, and we just can't see her."

"But she disappeared right before our eyes."

"Not right before our eyes, Paulo. The light was so bright we couldn't see anything, could we."

"That's true. Anything could have happened."

"Exactly."

Paulo ran over to the spot she had vanished from. There was no hole she could have fallen down. He looked up and all around. "Can't have been a transmat beam."

"Why do you say that?" the Captain said, running over to join him.

"Well you know that . . . I don't know how to describe it . . . that funny buzz in the air that puts goose pimples on your arms when there's just been a matter transfer."

"The residual energy lingering in the air after the subject's been removed from space."

He nodded. "Well it's not here, I can't sense it."♣

"You're right. Good observation, Paulo."

"Thank you, Captain."

"So if it wasn't matter transfer, or any other kind of teleportation . . ." he jumped up and down, "ground seems firm . . ."

"What else is there?"

"Either somebody just rushed over to her and grabbed her while we weren't looking . . . or something much more sinister is going on."

"Well there's not really any trees around where she could be hiding. Not for miles anyway."

"Evelyn!!" called the Captain, with his hands cupped around his mouth.

"She'd better not be playing a trick on us."

♣   Paulo knew all about matter transfer. The Satellite workers do a fair amount of it on Serothia.

"How would she have managed that? A full sound crew and professional pyrotechnics providing live special effects?"

"No," Paulo said, reflectively.

"She seemed . . . odd before she disappeared don't you think?"

"Odd? Yes, I suppose she did. She wasn't paying much attention to us and what was going on. She just wandered off."

"And she knows not to wander off."

"Perhaps we should wander off and look for her."

"But she can hardly have gone far . . . I suppose anything's possible. I'm always the first to admit that. Come on then."

The matron Evie was following came to a door at the end of a very drab and musty hallway. She opened it and led her in. The room beyond had a very different atmosphere from the hallway. It was brightly lit by the natural sunlight coming through the many large windows, and it would have been a very pleasant room, if it wasn't for the strange décor and the ridiculous music being played. It was supposed to be calming music, but its intention was so heavily exaggerated that it quickly became painful and sickly. The occupants of the room looked strange too. There were fourteen or fifteen of them, all between the age of thirty and sixty, and it looked as though they weren't bothered at all by the music. But what was really weird about them, was that some of them—grown men and women, were playing with doctor's-waiting-room-type toys. A few were staring out the window, and a couple of them were gazing at simple paintings on the wall. Then Evie felt really uncomfortable when she spotted two or three in different corners, doing nothing but sitting in a chair, staring blankly at the air in front of them.

"You'll be quite comfortable here, while you recover from your rest," said the matron.

Before Evie could stop her, the matron had closed the door—the matron outside and Evie stuck inside. She tried to open it back up herself, but it seemed to be locked. Evie took another look around the room. No one seemed to pay any attention to her. And if they did, it was just a simple look in her direction before they continued with their activity, (or non-activity). She walked straight over to a woman of about fifty something, sitting in a chair in the corner. She walked right in front of her, and then looked into her blank, staring face—and there was no response whatsoever.

"Hello?" she said softly.

Nothing.

She waved a hand in front of her face and said 'hello' again.

The woman slowly moved her head to face Evie. She was looking at her, yet her eyes didn't really appear to be *seeing* her. She smiled slightly—a brief, empty smile. Then Evie straightened up and took in the rest of the room. Looking at the woman any longer was too creepy.

Where am I? she thought to herself, starting to feel afraid. Then she knelt down beside a forty-something man who was on the floor playing with wooden blocks and said, "Where are we, please?"

He looked at her—his face much more lively, "The Sanctuary," he replied.

"How long have we been walking now?" called Paulo, starting to feel very tired. His feet were sore and his head felt like it was roasting in the afternoon sun.

The Captain looked at his very complicated-looking wrist watch.♣ "Almost thirty minutes."

"Feels longer than that. Feels like we've been wandering around for almost half an hour!"

"Half an hour is thirty . . ."

"Can we rest amongst these trees over here?" called Paulo.

"Alright, for a short while."

The Captain joined Paulo in the shade of a dozen or so trees. Paulo could see that the Captain was thinking very hard about something.

"What are you thinking?"

"Only how much I wish I still had my Unique Radio-Wave-Operated Link-Chip—and that I had one, and Evie had the other. Then we could track her."

"But even if it didn't get crushed underneath Mallory's foot, the other one wouldn't be in Evie's possession."

"I know. Just shows how being tired can cause one to think irrationally."

"You know, when I met you, I didn't think it was possible for you to get tired."

"Oh it is, Paulo. I'm just as human as you are."

"That reminds me," said Paulo, inclining his head to one side. "I don't actually know where you *are* from. I mean, are you from Earth like Evelyn? Or from yet another planet I haven't heard of. I know you're not from my planet."

"Well it's quite a long story, you see . . ."

♣   I think it did a lot more than just tell the time.

Before they knew it, there was shouting all around them. Men from all sides suddenly appeared from behind the trees holding spears and stones, and within seconds had the Captain and Paulo completely surrounded. They were wearing primitive clothing—stuff made from sheep skins and leaves and feathers and who knows what else. The most prominent shouter was right in front of Paulo and the Captain holding up a spear and dressed the most colourfully out of the whole mob. He also wore a large thick cape, made out of some kind of animal skin and he was well tanned.

At his signal, the mob stopped shouting. Without taking his eyes off the two stunned travellers, he inched toward them, step by step, always sustaining a defensive position.

To ease the apparent seriousness of the moment, the Captain nodded his head and said, "Afternoon. Lovely day."

"Grab them!!!" yelled the leader, and all of a sudden, four others had come forward from behind them and restrained their arms. There was no escape. The Captain saw in the eyes of the leader animal-like aggression and hostility. These ruffians were predators, and the Captain and Paulo appeared to have been trespassing on their territory.

Chapter Three

Home Sweet Home

A downhearted man walked slowly into the consulting room. He looked utterly lost, lonely and depressed—at the end of his rope. He was welcomed and led through a doorway by another man. This one was in a suit and tie—very upright and stiff, yet his face was beaming with a smile.

"Come this way, don't be afraid. Have a seat."

The downhearted man plonked down in an armchair opposite a desk. "My name's Mark," said the suited man. "Now what's troubling you? You just feel free to talk and I'll listen."

"Well," said the man, quietly, "my wife's left me."

"I see, and she's taken all your belongings and kept the house, that sort of thing?"

"Oh no, I have everything. She moved out. She doesn't want anything from me. But . . . I still love her madly, and I want her back. What can I do?"

"Well I can't get your wife back for you, I'm afraid. But I know exactly what you need."

"Oh? What's that?" the man asked through tears.

The suited man smiled tenderly, stood up and walked around to his client. "Come this way."

The man got up and followed the consultant.

In another room, a long way away, on another planet as a matter of fact, another man, sitting at a desk, was watching the whole situation going on right in front of him on a visual and audio monitor. "Yes," he was saying, "that's right. That's right. He needs us, the poor man."

The suited man opened a door to his client and invited him into an adjoining room. The door closed. Then locked. Due to all the sound-proof walls, the screeching could not be heard from outside.

"Look, what's the meaning of this?" said the Captain. "We're innocent. We haven't done anything to you. I can't imagine why you want to hold us prisoner! Unless of course we're your dinner." He erupted into laughter as he said it, but the capturers were not even smiling.

Suddenly the Captain and Paulo looked extremely worried. "We're . . . not your . . . dinner . . . are we?"

"Stop it, Captain," whispered Paulo. "You're giving them ideas."

"But that's illegal," said the Captain, staring back into the leader's cold, hard eyes.

"Calm yourself," the leader suddenly said, lowering his spear. "We are not cannibals."

The two breathed a sigh of relief.

"We must always detain any wanderers in order to evaluate their intentions, their hostility if any, and their reasons for being here."

The Captain paused, eyeing the leader and his troupe. "You speak very well."

"Will you state your intentions!"

"Well our intentions are to basically wander about to try and find a lost friend of ours, our hostility is nil . . . unless of course there is cause to be, and our reason for being here is simple. Something went wrong with our coordinates and . . . well, we took a wrong turn as they say."

"You're here by accident?"

"Yes we are," said Paulo.

"And you got here by your own space craft?"

Paulo was about to answer *yes*, but the Captain stopped him. "Er . . . we were in a way, dropped off here. By someone else who was flying the craft."*

"Why do you need to know, anyway?" asked Paulo.

"Well I suppose it doesn't matter," said the leader. Then he called out to the rest of his group. "Lay down your weapons. We will assist these unfortunate travellers." Then he made proper eye-contact with both the Captain and Paulo. This time, his eyes were friendly. "My name is Asher, and I think we may be able to help you."

"That's very decent of you. I'm the Captain, and this is my friend Paulo. And to be honest with you, some help is just what we need at the moment."

Evie would have gone mad if she hadn't decided to recite the periodic table over and over again. Sitting in this room, with these mad people, listening to this mad music, for a maddening amount of time . . . it was surely the periodic table that saved her. She wondered why she was the only person in the room noticing how weird it all was. Everyone else seemed to be a part of it—not a spectator like her.

---

*   It was due to past experience that caused the Captain to . . . bend the truth a little. Last time someone discovered he had a space ship of his own, it was stolen from him.

Someone finally came back into the room. Another young woman that was dressed like a nurse. She had called "D14" and hadn't got a response. The nurse looked straight into Evie's eyes as she called the second time. "D14!"

Then Evie remembered, *she* was D14—apparently. She stood up, looking at the nurse, still wondering whether it was her that she was calling. The nurse had nodded and raised her arm out in front of her, signaling Evie to come back out through the door.

"Why don't you just call me Evie, it's not that difficult to say, is it?"

The nurse hadn't replied. She gently nudged her as she passed through the doorway and led her right out of the building through a number of old wood paneled rooms and hallways. Finally, the open air! Evie breathed in a long, deep breath of it. It was so fresh and clean—as opposed to the stuffy, city air she was used to in Adelaide where she lived.

But she wasn't allowed to enjoy it for long; she was taken more or less straight back inside—into the back seat of an old-fashioned car painted pink and pale green. Then before she even got a look at the driver, the car took off along a winding road.

"Excuse me," Evie said, bravely, "where am I being taken to?"

She didn't actually expect a reply, but then it came: "Home, Miss."

She frowned, utterly confused. "Home?"

The drive was pleasant. They drove past some nice looking houses and country-village-style shops. There were trees either side of the road much of the time and a nice mild breeze through the air. Except, the pleasant ride was tainted by Evie's feelings of confusion, and her fear of being all by herself in a strange place. Nothing familiar; everyone and everything strange and different . . . until . . .

The car veered slowly around the last corner of the trip and suddenly, there was her house. Evie's home in Adelaide . . . Australia . . . Earth!

Evie's mouth dropped open as she stared out at it. "I really *am* home," she heard herself say.

"Of course, Miss," said the driver.

Everything was just the way it was when she last saw it. The half finished paint job on the front fence, the petunias she helped her mum plant just the other day, the silky oak and gum leaves still lying all over the front lawn that Mum had pestered Dad to rake up. The only differences were that there were no immediate neighbouring houses, and instead of it saying number twenty-seven on the letterbox, it said *D14.*

Evie was slowly getting out of the car, and as soon as she closed the car door behind her, while still staring at the house, the car drove off in a flash.

Evie looked all around her. The surroundings were not right. But her house was. It was as if some big claw on a crane had picked up her home from Adelaide—garden and all and plonked it down here. She opened the gate and ran up the path to the front door. The lights were on inside, but all was quiet. She opened the door, and seeing her house again after travelling with the Captain was strange. Even though it had felt like she'd been away for weeks and weeks, seen other worlds and met people from ancient times; now, it was like she was just coming home from a day at school.

She called up the hallway, still with a frown, "Mum!?"

She looked into the lounge room. "Mum?"

She jogged up the hallway a bit. "Dad?"

She called down the hallway towards her brother's room. "James?"

Then she ran through the kitchen and out to the back yard (which was incidentally all exactly how it was when she left it too). "Is anybody here? Hello!?"

She came back inside—into the silence. She knew this couldn't be real, but she had caught herself, wishing, even half expecting that her family would be here. But she did soon realise that she was quite alone.

"So what are *you* doing here?" the Captain asked Asher, while they were walking along the terrain.

The group had been walking for a while now, and the land had changed from looking like a lush, green countryside, to more of a dry, rocky one.

"We're existing," replied Asher. "Trying to survive. There's not much on this planet to support life outside the Sanctuary."

"What's the Sanctuary?"

"The Sanctuary? It's the main purpose of this planet. The only reason you'd come here is if you're destined for the Sanctuary."

"But what is it?" said Paulo. "*Where* is it? Maybe Evie's there."

"I have no doubt she's there," said Asher. "She wouldn't survive long on her own if she wasn't in the Sanctuary."

"But to look at this place," said the Captain, "one would think it's teeming with resources. All those living trees and the fresh grass back there. Surely there's plenty of flora and fauna to live off."

"It is a strange place. The seasons are crazy and the land is unpredictable. We have found enough to serve our needs around the place, but it's been hard. In the forestland at night, for example, there is no rest or adequate shelter there. It teems with life alright. Beasts that are more powerful predators than us. They could rip you apart in the blink of an eye. So finding shelter at night is near impossible. You're often safer out in the open.

"Tell me more about this Sanctuary place," said the Captain.

"Sounds like the place to be if you're stranded out here," said Paulo.

"On the contrary," Asher said, harshly. "I'd rather be out here, fighting to stay alive than in the Sanctuary. You see, my friends and I . . . we're looking to get *off* this planet. We're trying to get as far away from the Sanctuary as possible."

Chapter Four

The Bubble

Evie flopped down into her favourite couch in the lounge room. She loved it because it was so soft and spongy, she use to never want to leave it when her mum would say, 'bedtime'. She grabbed the remote control from the arm and switched on the T.V. Nothing interesting was on. There were no recognisable television stations. One that was the most boring of them all, was a man talking. He was talking as if he was some kind of political leader. His head was balding and his most noticeable feature was his large nose, with a rosy, bulbous tip. She switched it off, and got up. It was the same kind of chair physically, but she would never be able to feel as comfortable in it, knowing that it must be merely a copy of the one in her real house.

This whole place is a copy, isn't it? she thought. *It must be.* She went up the hall and entered her own bedroom. How nice it was to see it again. Once again, everything was as it was when she left it—to the last detail. Everything from the ball of blue tack she had stuck on her wall next to her ultra-messy desk, to the three pairs of socks on the floor that she hadn't put in the wash basket yet.

How can this be? She went over to her desk and picked up her diary. She thought she might carry it around with her and write about all her recent adventures. When she opened it up however, there was nothing written in it so far. She knew she'd written stuff in there before. She was so certain of it because she was always so angry at James when he'd pick it up and read stuff from it. But this one, it was empty—even though the front of it was exactly the same.*

Then she opened the top drawer to get a pen out. There was nothing in the drawer! Now usually she'd have trouble even opening it because of all the things she'd stuffed in there . . . but all the drawers were empty. She kept hold of her diary, and ran around the whole house, opening drawers and cupboards and boxes and wardrobes. All of them empty! The only wardrobe that had a few things in it was James'. But Evie was careful to notice that his wardrobe had already been ajar. Under the beds were vacant and bottom sheets were plain white when she knew her own were pink with white spots. Book covers were all complete and detailed but inside them were blank. The kitchen cupboards and drawers were empty and the fridge too, was empty. (Even though all the correct photographs and magnets were there, stuck on the front.)

It was then that Evie knew, it was all for show. Nothing was real. It was like a photograph. The only details you're given is what you can see, without moving or opening anything. While gazing around the kitchen, she suddenly noticed something that wasn't an original

---

* She'd decorated it herself with brown paper underneath and then tissue paper and ribbon, and drawn patterns.

item in her own house—something out of place. It was a leaflet on the kitchen cupboard-top, next to the tea and coffee canisters. She went to it, and picked it up. On the front, it said *The Sanctuary*, and in it were listed all sorts of different shops and facilities and their location on a map.

> *The Sanctuary Square:*
> *The Sanctuary Convenience Store*
> *The Sanctuary Café*
> *The Sanctuary Chemist*
> *The Sanctuary Hair Salon*
>
> *Other places of interest:*
> *The Sanctuary Cinema*
> *The Sanctuary Art Gallery*

The list went on. Evie put it inside her pocket, and decided to leave the house. It was too weird being there and she'd had enough of it for the time being. So she left to look for the Sanctuary Square.

"We came from the Sanctuary," said Asher, while the group was still trekking across the land.

"Not originally, you understand," said another. "We all lived there for a time."

"At different times," said Asher. "And at different times, we all got away, met up on the outside and now we're trying to survive out here. Living off the earth."

"This planet isn't called Earth though is it?" said the Captain.

"We wouldn't have a clue what this planet is called. We're not here by choice, you know. I'm from a planet

29

called Zoran. Elsa here is from Maltor, Jon and Pintz, they're both from Sharr . . ."

"Those worlds all have billions of light-years between them!" said the Captain, stunned.

"You know them then?"

"I've heard of them, yes. Their positions in the cosmos are very wide spread. How did you come to be here in one place?"

"We were all brought here," said Elsa.

"But not this spot specifically," said Asher. "We were brought to *the Sanctuary*."

"By whom?"

"By a very large and powerful influence."

It wasn't all that far to walk until Evie came to a more populated part of this place she'd been brought to. Up ahead, was like an old market square of a small country village. At first, she smiled. It looked pleasant. Peaceful atmosphere, friendly people, dainty tables and chairs outside what looked like the café.

She walked up to a girl who was clearing away a cup and a plate from one of the tables.

"Is this the Sanctuary Café?" she asked timidly.

"Sure is," the girl replied with a smile. "Why don't you pull up a chair and sit down? I'll bring you a menu."

The girl disappeared into the café, so Evie, looking cautiously around, sat down. It was a gorgeous day!

Soon, the girl was back with a menu. It all looked very simple. Tea, coffee, milkshakes, juices, toasted sandwiches, chocolate cake. She looked up from the menu and saw a lady at another table opposite, also looking over the menu. Evie decided to be brave and go and talk to her.

"I'm new here," Evie said, "what's the nicest thing to eat?"

"The tuna and salad baguette I think. It's what I always get," the woman said kindly.

"I don't like tuna much."

"Well you'd better not get it then. Perhaps the chicken one."

"How long have you been here?"

"Oh, um . . . it would be about er . . . ha, do you know something, I can't remember. That's how wonderful this place is. Makes you forget all your troubles."

"Where abouts do you live?"

"Across the square a little way, down the lane and opposite those big palm trees."

"Do you like it here?"

"Like it? Of course I do. It's so peaceful and relaxing. Don't you agree?"

". . . Yes, it's peaceful and relaxing alright. I just don't know how I got here."

"Oh don't worry about that. Just think about how care-free your life will be now that you are here."

"What were you doing before you came here?"

"Oh I was . . . some sort of instructor. I taught little people all sorts of things—spelling, grammar, science and, what is it they call . . . er . . . ma . . . math . . . mathematics, that's the word."

"You were a school teacher?"

"Yes, that sounds about right. So stressful at times! Busy busy busy, all the time, not a moment to myself. I knew I had to do something about it."

"And now you're here."

"Exactly."

"What do you do here?"

"What do you mean, what do I do here?"

"What do you do for a job, for a living? Are you still teaching?"

"Teaching? Are you joking? I do nothing. I'm a lady of leisure. Have been for years and years and years."

Evie looked at her and thought she didn't look old enough to have been a teacher and then have stopped years and years and years ago. She frowned in confusion.

The waitress of the café came over to the table. "Have you decided?"

"I don't have any money," replied Evie.

"Money? Just tell me your code, sweet."

"Code? Um . . . oh, D14 . . . I think."

"Right, what would you like?"

"Chicken and salad baguette?"

"And I'll have the tuna thanks F67," said the other lady.

"Fine. Won't be long." She smiled and walked briskly off with their orders written down on a pad.

"So you're D14," said the woman. "It's nice to meet your acquaintance. I'm 81C3."

Evie repeated slowly and in a quandary, "81 . . . C3?"

"Yes, the Sanctuary is wonderful," she sighed, looking up to the sky and soaking up the sun. "I've almost completely forgotten all that stress in my life that I had to endure before you mentioned it."

Evie was still frowning. She guessed that 81C3 had perhaps almost completely forgotten not just her stress, but her whole life as well.

The group had been walking over the rocky hill country for a long while, and Asher had said they were heading for the jungle region as soon as possible.

"Why do we need to reach the jungle region," Paulo asked.

"Because the sun is getting lower in the sky, and we still have no meal for tonight. We must hunt for food now or we go hungry. The Jungle region is the most likely place to find prey."

"Hunt?" Paulo said, alarmed. "I'm not a hunter."

"You do not have to accompany us, but there is no guarantee that we will come back this way to collect you once the deed is done."

"We will accompany you," said the Captain. "Only we're not very experienced in . . . such activity. We hope you'll be generous enough . . ."

"Do not worry. Even if you do not contribute to the catch, I'm sure there will be plenty of it to share with you."

"That's very decent of you, thank you." The Captain did not fancy himself as much of a hunter. He could fish. In fact, he was a very good fisherman—in a number of ways, but hunting . . . well, I'll just say that this was a first for him. Yes, even for such a person as the Captain.

"Captain," Paulo whispered to him without the others noticing. "we won't have to eat raw meat will we? I don't think I could eat raw meat."

"I'm sure they have the resources necessary to cook it," said the Captain. "I mean, it's not like they're cave men and haven't discovered how to make fire yet. No, I'm *sure* they'll cook it . . . I hope."

Evie guessed it was around three or four in the afternoon. She was finishing off her chicken baguette, which turned out to be very nice, and she'd just said goodbye to 81C3 who left to do some leisurely shopping.

After taking her last bite, Evie glanced around the café again—at all the people sitting on the outside tables and then all the people sitting at tables inside the building. They all had that same relaxed, burden-free look on their faces as the woman did. Even though it was a peaceful atmosphere, there wasn't a lot of chit chat around the place—not a lot of fellowship. Everyone seemed to be on their own, in their own little world, soaking up the joys of their own empty, nothingness leisure. Although they all seemed content, it disturbed Evie. But she couldn't quite describe why in her mind. She was confused as to why she wasn't finding it absolute heaven—having nothing to do and no responsibilities to worry about.

She turned back around to her own little table to finish the last sip of her orange juice and jumped of fright. There was a man sitting opposite her at the same table.

"Good afternoon, D14. It's a pleasure to finally welcome you personally to your new home."

Evie soon recognised him as the man she'd seen on the T.V. The one with the balding hair and the big nose. He was smiling, but he gave her the creeps straight away.

"Who are you?"

"I am called A1. I trust you have settled in well, and that your home is comfortable."

"It's not my home."

He inclined his head to one side and simply said, "Mmm. Interesting."

"Well it looks like it. But it's not."

"Very interesting."

"Why am I here?" she asked timidly. But then she added with a little more aggression, "And how did you know what my house looks like?"

"Oh it was nothing," he said calmly, with a modest smile, "you can thank me later. All I wanted to do for the time being was welcome you and let you know that all of this . . ." he signaled the café, the shops, the gardens and everything, "is as good as yours. It's your home—enjoy it."

"But . . ."

"When I say *yours*, I mean it's still a public place, so you can't go round vandalising it or anything." He laughed, but Evie didn't. She was too afraid.

"Make yourself at home. Make some friends. And if there's anything you need, just drop a little note in the suggestion box in the village square, okay." He spoke like a posh upstart—a deep, commanding, but hospitable voice.

Evie looked at all her surroundings again saying, "But, what is all this? Where am I and how did I get here?"

When she looked back to demand an answer from the man . . . he was gone.

The group of hunters, along with Paulo and the Captain, had reached the outskirts of a jungle-like location.

"This place *is* amazing," said Paulo on the quiet to the Captain. "One minute we're travelling across a desert and the next, we're in a jungle paradise."

There was a loud shriek coming from above them—high up in the trees. It made them jump. It was some native animal going about its most ordinary business.

"This place may *look* like a paradise," replied the Captain, "but I have a feeling, it's quite the opposite."

The moment they were deeper into the jungle, anybody would be able to sense, that danger lurked everywhere.

"Stay close," said Asher to the whole group. "A big group looks more threatening to any possible predator."

"You mean, *we* are prey as well?" said Paulo, beginning to feel a cold shiver down his spine.

"In this jungle, anything is prey," said Asher. "We are not yet certain who or what is at the top of the food chain on this planet."

"What do you normally go for?" asked the Captain.

"We normally find plenty of jungle birds, quite often grey foxes. But I would love, just once, to catch a Mandrera Cat."

"What's that then?"

"A large vicious beast—looks like it's from the cat family. Short fur of bright orange and black stripes!"

"Sounds like a tiger."

"T-t-tiger?" shuddered Paulo.

"Quite possibly you have a different name for such creatures," Asher was saying to the Captain. "We have merely invented the names of all the animals and creatures seen on this planet. We don't know any better."

"That would explain the grey fox. I've never heard of a fox living in the jungle."

"Shhh," Asher commanded.

The group, led by Asher, moved slowly forward. By the looks of it, they were experienced hunters. They moved just like a single lioness, creeping along through the grass so slowly, one could hardly notice any movement at all. One step at a time, each a deep lunge so that at any moment, they were ready to spring off their feet to pounce . . . or run away.

Paulo couldn't see anything—nor could the Captain, but the group of experts had obviously sensed something nearby, worth exploring. The noises of the jungle were unnerving Paulo, and he gently touched the Captain on the arm.

The Captain jumped with fright, almost disturbing the team of hunters. When he realised it was only Paulo at his elbow, he sighed and whispered, "What is it?"

"Well . . . aren't tigers man-eating monsters? I read about them in Intergalactic Geography."

"Just stay with the group, they seem to know what they're doing."

"But we're not armed with anything."

"I know." The Captain seemed slightly worried himself. "Even Bungalow Bill took an elephant and a gun. And in case of accidents he always took his mum."

"What? Who's he?"

"Never mind. Only trying to relax my nerves a bit." They kept on following close behind the hunters. "I know," the Captain said next, "Just think about my friend I've been telling you about, remember?"♣

"You mean the one called Jesus. The Baby in the stable? The one Evie said turned an ocean into dry land?"

"Yes. And many other things. He'll protect us if we just trust."

♣ This was one of the reasons why Paulo had asked to travel with the Captain. To learn more about a mysterious friend of the Captain's that he'd kept mentioning.

"But I didn't see him turn the ocean into dry land. When was this?"

"What about when he made ten minutes seem like hours and all those people on Satellite SB-17 were saved. You were there then."♣

"I suppose that was kind of weird."

"Not weird, Paulo. Miraculous!"

"Will you keep it quiet back there!" Asher said in a raspy whisper.

Just then, there was a growling sound not too far away. The Captain and Paulo looked at each other. The Captain knew that Paulo, using a look rather than words, was asking whether that was the growl of a tiger. He nodded to him with wide, alert eyes.

"The Cat!" Asher whispered to the others. "Conceal yourself. Be ready to strike. I'll lure it over here!"

The Captain could hardly believe a group of mere humans could bring down a tiger. He hid like the rest of them, and hoped that the tiger himself was not as hungry as he was.

Asher called out in his raspy whisper again, "Captain! What does your friend think he's doing?"

The Captain looked out at the clearing, where Paulo was standing by himself, with his eyes closed. The Captain smiled to himself, "Trusting," he said and went out there to fetch him. "Take cover man."

"Whoops!" I don't think Paulo realised everybody had left to find a hiding spot, because he looked all around him, suddenly realizing he was alone. While doing so,

---

♣   Satellite SB-17 was where Paulo worked before he met the Captain. They had ten minutes to evacuate fifteen hundred people from the Satellite—six at a time—before it exploded.

he saw a flash of orange and black through the trees on the other side of the clearing. He gasped and made a run for it out of the clearing, towards the Captain, but on his forth step, he tripped over a thick tree root which was sticking up out of the ground. He heard the tiger's padding paw-steps pounding against the soft, damp jungle soil.

"Paulo!" the Captain yelled out.

As Paulo tumbled to the ground—the tiger only metres away and now in full view of the hunters—there was a loud *jangle!* and a *clatter, bang, rattle, CLANG!* and the tiger, as though it was a jumpy, frightened little kitten, scampered away into the thick of the jungle.

There lay Paulo, stretched out on his belly, surrounded by an assortment of metal tools that had fallen out of his overall pockets when he'd fallen.

"What happened?" he said as he tried to pick himself up.

"You scared him off, that's what happened!" said Asher, irritated.

"Pardon me, but that tiger was seconds away from killing Paulo. And after it killed him, he would have moved on to all of you, so you owe him some thanks."

"We would have caught him eventually," said Asher.

"Yes, but at the expense of how many lives? I thought the purpose of hunting was to sustain life. Have you ever tried catching a Mer . . . whatever-you-call-it-cat before and realised how powerful they are?"

". . . No."

"Then I advise you to leave them alone in future for your sake and stick to the grey fox."

Asher opened his mouth to speak, but the Captain cut him off.

"And don't say it would be for pride's sake if you caught one one day. Otherwise you'll turn into rich snobbish so and soes who hunt for trophies rather than food. And if you'll take the time to notice," he said while helping Paulo gather up all the tools, "I think you'll find your dinner laying on the ground over there." He signaled to the other side of the clearing with his head. They all looked, including Paulo.

It was a smallish furry creature, already dead.

"A grey fox," said one of the hunters.

"It was part of the tiger's kill, but since he left rather unexpectedly, I'm sure we could help ourselves."

They all walked over to view it and Asher picked it up. "It will be enough for our needs tonight," he admitted.

The Captain led the way out of there, and on his way past Asher, he said without stopping, "That's a large Terafian Short-Tailed Squirrel, by the way."

It didn't take long for Evie to get fed up with people. Everywhere she looked, there was at least somebody with a silly contented smile on their face. There was no doubt about it, it was a peaceful, content sort of place, but she just didn't feel like joining in. The way that woman talked of her previous life—it was like she had to really think about it to remember any of it. It wasn't like that for Evie, and she didn't ever want it to be.

In her mind, she considered going back to her 'home' to get away from people. But she remembered how she'd felt when she was there—all she wanted to do was get out.

So she decided to keep on walking around, and not stop until she got away from people. Was that even possible? she thought. Was it even a good idea? The sun had almost completely disappeared from the horizon, which she could see through a row of pine trees. She'd never been for a walk on her own at this time of day back home. She considered for a while, and then kept on walking. She walked and she walked and she walked, enjoying the scenery, but also looking for some clue as to where in the world . . . (correction: *universe*) she was.

The sun was setting, and one of Asher's friends was cooking up the squirrel. It didn't look like the most wonderful meat, but the group was hungry, so it didn't matter very much.

"How did you know what that animal was called, Captain?" asked Paulo, privately—away from Asher and his friends. "If you know the animal, you must know what planet this is."

"Unfortunately no, I haven't been able to narrow it down to one planet. If I'm right about the squirrel, we're in the galaxy T47 or as it's more commonly known: the 'Swan Neck Galaxy'. Lots of Terafian animals can be found all throughout certain regions of the galaxy. Terafian simply means (in Swan Neck Galaxy terms) nocturnal animals that have fur but lay eggs, rather than give birth to live young. I learnt that in *my* Intergalactic Geography classes."

"I see. Thanks for sticking up for me about the tiger, Captain."

"Well, that Asher was getting on my nerves. And speaking of which, there's still some information I want from him."

Later, while they were eating, the Captain did not hesitate to bring the Sanctuary back up into the conversation.

"What do you mean you 'got away'?" he asked, taking a bite out of a small portion of the dry meat.

"Got away? When did I say that?"

"Earlier today, you said all of you have 'got away' from the Sanctuary. Do you mean you escaped?"

"Of course. You have to escape. They don't let you *walk* out."

"What kind of a place is this Sanctuary?" asked Paulo.

"Haven't you got the gist yet? It's as good as a prison. We are *escaped prisoners.*"

Evie was finally free of people, and she wasn't sure whether it was because it was now quite dark, or because of how far she'd walked. She hoped it was the latter. If she had to stay in this weird place for long, she would come here often.

She'd walked up quite a steady hill, and now when she looked out ahead of her, all she saw was wide, open country side. She could see quite clearly a few yards in front of her, but off to the distance, it got pretty dark, because the sun was setting in the opposite direction.

She had a thought that maybe it was the same countryside where she got lost in the first place. *This must be the way I came in. And therefore, it must be the way out!* she thought to herself. *If they haven't done something silly and wandered off, the Captain and Paulo should be out there somewhere wondering where I've got to.*

There was no sign of anyone, but she knew there was no point in hesitating. She started walking again, setting off in a straight line forwards. But something funny happened. She soon felt a sort of gentle, barely noticeable pushing behind her left shoulder, and when she took one step after another, intending for them to go straight forward, she seemed to be turning around by her right shoulder. When she looked up again, all she saw in front of her was . . . the Sanctuary. She had a good view of it from a height because of the hill she'd climbed.

It was like a weird dream. *But I was sure I was facing away from it.* She turned around 180° on the spot and tried walking away from the Sanctuary again—out towards the bare grassy hilltops. Again, that strange gentle nudging feeling behind her left shoulder, and all she was doing was walking towards the Sanctuary again.

She tried numerous times, but it was the same outcome every time. It was like there was an invisible bubble as a wall—when you try and walk into it, your shoulder slides along it's flexible curvature and there is nowhere else for your feet to go, but to the side, and then back the way you came.

Evie was becoming frustrated. All that was ahead of her was the Sanctuary. She could see the roof tops of houses and shops, the narrow winding streets, and all the trees lining them. She could see roads leading towards the beach and big buildings she assumed to be the Museum and Art Gallery and so on. It was all just the Sanctuary as far as the eye could see. The Sanctuary. The Sanctuary. The Sanctuary.

Next thing, something violently grabbed both her arms and she was yanked away from the spot. She saw a flash of two or three figures dressed in black—masks and gloves and all. She felt herself being lowered down onto what felt like a hard plank of wood. And since that's the last thing she remembered, I'll fill you in on the rest. The hard plank of wood was a carrier-bed. There were four men carrying her—one on each corner, and they trotted her off down the hill, back into the happy little village known as the Sanctuary.

Chapter Five

Enter Or Exit?

When Evie could finally open her eyes,* she just saw ceiling again. A drab and boring ceiling and a very long way away. In fact, it could almost be described as distant.

"Good morning," said a voice. It was cold and dispassionate.

Evie jumped and jerked her head up to see who it was with her in the room. Sitting right next to her in a chair was a suited man—short, stout, with glasses and black thinning hair, and resting a clipboard on his lap.

Evie herself discovered she was in a chair like at the dentist—half sitting up, half lying down. This made her very uncomfortable and she tried getting up, but she didn't seem to have control over her limbs yet.

"Lay back and relax D14," said the man. "It's for your own good. If you try and get up and move around now, you'll only go and hurt yourself."

Evie then tried to speak, but even her mouth and vocal chords wouldn't work properly yet.

---

* She had, before this, made several attempts but could not seem to budge them due to grogginess.

"Now, my name is Mark," said the man in a slightly more gentle tone. "You've simply been given a form of sedative so that I can talk to you without any unpleasantness."

It was too much hard work to stay sitting up, so Evie had no choice but to lie back down and listen to the guy.

"Now, D14," Mark began, using a calm, patient voice. "Why did you try and escape?"

Evie just frowned and moaned a little.

The man in the chair leant to one side where some controls were. He slid one little knob along about two centimetres. "I think you'll find you can talk now," he said with a vacant smile.

It was strange that when Evie tried to talk now, she was able to—just like the man said. "I didn't," she simply said.

"Why did you try to escape, D14?"

"I wasn't trying to escape."

"What were you doing so far from the Sanctuary Square?"

"I was walking."

"We know. But why so far?"

"I felt like a nice long walk."

"Why is that?"

"I don't know. To get away from the people."

"So you were making an escape of a kind, weren't you."

"Well . . ."

"Weren't you, D14?" He spoke to her like a head-master would to a naughty schoolgirl who should know better.

"I suppose. But how can you escape *from* a place that many people have said they've escaped *to*?"

One of the man's eyebrows rose up with interest.

"Why did *you* come here, D14?"

"I didn't come here. I think I was kidnapped."

The man laughed. It was a soft and gentle laugh—but so sinister. "I'll ask again. Why did you come to the Sanctuary?"

"I don't have a reason. As I said, I was brought here. It wasn't my choice to come."

"By whom?"

"I haven't got a clue. Maybe that man, that . . . A1, I don't know."

"D14, people come here because they are stressed and in need of a break—an *escape* as you put it. They find themselves here to get away from it all. To relax and enjoy the good life. Now why do you suppose you're here?"

"I told you, I don't know."

"You can't think of any reason why you'd like to escape your everyday life back home? Your brother James perhaps . . ."

"How do you know about James?"

". . . Have you two been arguing? Were you getting too fed up with him *and* having to worry about your schoolwork at the same time? When you fight with him, he just doesn't understand how you're feeling, does he? The whole family for that matter."

"Look, this is all rubbish, I don't know how . . ."

"How about that time you were doing some homework on your brother's computer and you left it to go and get a drink."

Evie was struck speechless.

"You came back and your brother was on the computer and said something like . . ."

"*You had something important on here didn't you*," Evie said it with him.

"Something had gone wrong with the computer, you lost your work and you began to shout at James."

"It wasn't his fault."

"No. You were just angry at the world, that's all. You stormed all over the house and made everybody afraid to come near you."

With a tear rolling past her ear, Evie said, "All James said was *you should have saved it*."

"And that's not what you needed to hear was it. You already knew that. All you wanted to know—all you needed to know, was that somebody understood how you were *feeling*. By now, you're not just angry because you've lost some work you'd been doing on the computer, but because of the very fact that you've become so angry and lost your temper."

Evie turned onto her side, to face the man in the chair. "Yes!" she said. "That's exactly it."

"You didn't *want* to be in a bad mood. And because you've lost your temper, nobody wants to come near you, but all you need right now is your mother to hug you."

"Yes!"

"It's times like that you'd like to escape, wouldn't you?"

"Yes," replied Evie.

"It's times like that you realise how ridiculous life is. How unhappy it can be."

"Yes."

"How unhappy *you are* . . . deep down inside."

She wriggled back onto her back staring at the ceiling again and sighed. "Yes . . ." She thought of her mum, her dad, James.

"Wouldn't you just love to leave it all behind—forget it all? And live completely . . . stress free . . . ?"

She thought of their smiles. Mum's hugs. James' jokes. Dad's laugh. She looked back sharply at the man with the clipboard. "Of course not!" She felt power in her arms and legs. "They're my family! I love them!" She stood up from the chair, found the door and stormed out of the room.

Mark looked down sadly at his clipboard and put a big strike through the middle of the piece of paper resting on it. He then looked up in the general direction of a far wall and said out loud, "D14 interview unsuccessful. She'll be heading for the exit."

Then came a different voice, in reply: "Let her leave. We'll see her again soon."

Evie recognised some of the hallways on her way out of that huge room. It was enough to find her way out of the building and once again, she was so glad of the fresh air. There was commotion just outside the Infirmary though. There were four men dressed in black dragging a tall girl along the ground towards the big front entrance. She was yelling at them and kicking and pushing to try and get free. On their way past, Evie and the girl's eyes met for a split second. And in that split second, Evie got a slightly bigger glimpse of this place. Here was someone else they were about to interrogate, just like she had been. The thing that got to Evie the most though was the fact that she was the only person that seemed to be paying any attention to the commotion. Any other bystanders seemed to be unsurprised by it—completely unfussed by the whole scene. She felt dizzy with frustration.

The Captain and Paulo camped through the night with Asher and the other escapees. They had lots of hand-made blankets and the knowledge of good warm places to sleep. Without them, the Captain feared what would have become of both him and Paulo. After they had all arisen early in the day and had some good old bush tucker for breakfast,* the Captain was eager to get on with his and Paulo's mission, which was to find Evie. He imagined that from now on, he and Paulo would have to go on alone in search of her, but when he brought up the subject, a rather different turn of events seemed to come about.

"Right," he said, slapping his knees and getting up off the rock he was sitting on. "I can't thank you all enough for helping us and sharing your food with us, but I would like to cut to the chase now."

"Explain your meaning."

"Um . . . get to the point?"

"Point at what?"

"No not point at something, I mean the point of me being here . . . *purpose*. I have to find my friend, Evelyn."

"And you're sure she's in the Sanctuary?"

"No."

"What if she's lost in the jungle?" asked Paulo.

---

* An Australian term for natural foods found in the wild—the Australian bush. Though in this particular wild, I suppose you'd call it jungle tucker.

"Or the swamp lands?" asked another of the escapees.

"Or the forest?"

"Or the desert?"

"She disappeared almost in front of our eyes yesterday, remember," the Captain said to Paulo. Then he faced Asher. "That's why I'm quite sure she didn't just wander off. But that she was *taken*."

"Sounds like the Sanctuary for sure," said Asher. "And this is where I think you'll be a help to us as well as us providing help for you."

"What do you mean?"

"You've given me motivation."

"Motivation?"

"For weeks, I've been thinking about the Sanctuary—about all those people still living there. Most of them don't have any consciousness of what they're doing there and how they even got there. Something has to be done, but there's always a thought in the back of our minds, that if we got ourselves back in there—we may not get out again."

". . . And?" The Captain waited for the explanation of how this involved him.

"Well, you're an intelligent looking being . . ."

(The Captain gave a small, modest smile.)

". . . and I believe that if we joined forces, we'd surely come to a good plan."

"To get inside the Sanctuary?"

"Surely yes, but we won't stop there! To over-throw A1's power—(that's the man in charge). We'll take over the place and set everybody free!"

The Captain was speechless for a short moment. "That's quite ambitious."

"I know. And dangerous. But I would go in a second if I knew I had help."

The Captain considered and looked back at Paulo, who was standing a little behind him.

"If it's our only chance of finding Evie," he said.

Then the Captain turned to Asher. "Let's do it. But I can't see how I'd be much of a help. I mean, you know far more about this place than I do."

"Don't worry. I'm just glad of another companion." He looked at Paulo. "Another *two* companions—I hope."

Paulo nodded. "Yes, I'm in."

"How many, of your group, are prepared to join us?"

"There is a handful who have expressed their willingness to do such a thing. Jon and Pintz are up to it. Roscoe, Marnya and Elsa suggested their enthusiasm the other day. I know not of any others. We'll have to have a meeting."

"Friends," Asher announced to his group later, when he had assembled them all together and finally got their attention. He planted himself up on a big rock and spoke from this height—like standing on a pedestal to make a speech. He really looked the part of a brave tribe leader in all his animal skins and feathers. "We are about to embark* on a very important mission. One that has been pressing on my mind for some time. With the help of our

---

* Embark means to carry out or enter into. Not, as some commonly believe, to reproduce a sound resembling that of a dog.

new companions, it is our intention to go back into the Sanctuary . . ."

(At this, there were various gasps and mutterings from the listening group.)

". . . and put things right so that no one else will have to go through what we have gone through. For obvious reasons this is a dangerous mission—but necessary. The reason I am telling you is that it is the direction in which I would like to encourage you all to take. If you choose not to take it, you will from now on be on your own, since I, your leader will no longer be with you. But if you choose to come, it is possible your names will go down in history for this act of courage and service. I need to know now, who among you is willing to join me, knowing full well the risks involved."

Sure enough, Jon and Pintz came forward and stood with Paulo and the Captain, beside the rock that Asher was standing on. Another one soon came forward—a young woman, and Asher referred to her as Marnya. There then was a long period of time where nobody else came forward. Asher was beginning to look almost saddened. "Roscoe, Elsa? Will you not be part of this expedition? Thomas," he said to another.

"I doubt you'll ever make it in there, let alone get back out again!" Thomas replied.

"But if we achieve our goal, we'll be able to *walk* out of there! Macsus?" he addressed yet another.

"I think you're crazy!" Macsus called out. "You don't stand a chance. You'll get in there only to be traced, captured and patched again!"

"It's too dangerous," said someone else. "I just want to stick to our original mission and find a way off this planet!"

"She's right! Our chances are too slim."

"I'll join you!" called another woman. It was Elsa.

"And so will I!" said Roscoe finally, stepping forward. "It's worth the risk!"

"Well done!" cried Asher. "I knew I could rely on you. Now, will nobody else come with us? The more we have, the better our chances of success!"

But there was nobody else.

"Right," Asher said after a long pause. "We will set off in an hour exactly." ⁂

He stepped off his pedestal and started talking to his smaller group of brave volunteers.

The whole time, the Captain was thinking . . . *What a roundabout way of saying "I'm going on a dangerous mission—who wants to come with me?"*

So the brave little group of willing and able rescuers were as follows:

The Captain and Paulo of course, and Asher—tall, tanned and determined. Jon, who was quite a specimen of strength, fitness and masculine good looks. Pintz, a shorter man and wider around the middle. He had an honest face and the eyes of a loyal old sheep dog. Marnya was quite beautiful. She had long, dark hair, tanned skin from the sun (as all of them did), and she looked just as tough and determined as Asher. Roscoe was an older man, his hair graying at the sides and he couldn't walk as fast as the others. The environment had forced him to

---

⁂ After living in the wild for a while, with no clocks and no watches of any kind—no, not even the odd grandfather clock up next to the odd fir tree—they developed a rather clever way of telling time and judging amounts of time by the position of the sun in the sky.

keep fit however, and he had a kind smile. The last, was Elsa, a woman with a very vague face—one that could easily be forgotten in one's mind. She only looked thirty something, but her hair was white and short and she never really 'walked', but hobbled instead.

They all wore similar clothing. It was obvious they had on remnants of their ordinary street clothes from when they lived in the Sanctuary, but they were torn in places, and some holes and tears were patched up with materials from the environment.

Asher had said 'an hour' because his people had to gather up and pack necessary supplies, but the Captain was starting to feel restless. He just wanted to get started!

Chapter Six

The Conspiracy

As a tall pencil of a woman called Sue in a black skirt suit moved around her desk to approach another of her depressed clients, A1 was sitting in an oversized, over-computerised office, watching Evelyn passing through the streets on a huge screen planted up on the wall.

She looks puzzled, perplexed and perturbed. Her eyes are darting everywhere, looking suspiciously at the most mundane things. She's looking up, as if inspecting the sky. She looks at the faces of passers by, searching for any sign of emotions similar to hers. She turns around on herself. She doesn't know where she's going. She's seen someone—recognised them? She's walking towards . . . a girl . . . 7B12.

"Excuse me . . ." said Evie. "Are you the girl I saw being dragged into the Infirmary place earlier?"

The girl turned around and looked down at Evie—(she was a little taller than her). "Yes," she replied with hardly any expression. Yet at the same time, it seemed to be untrusting and cautious. "Who wants to know?" she added in the same manner, facing Evie square on. She had an American accent.

"Sorry, I was just . . . wondering er . . . I was standing outside the Infirmary at the time."

"Yeah, I noticed you." There was a pause. "Who are you?"

"Ev . . . er, D14."

The girl's eyes did a quick dart about and then fixed back on Evie and narrowed a little.

There was another pause. I think they were both waiting for the other one to say something.

It was the American girl who finally spoke next. "Well, if you don't mind, I'll be getting home. Have a nice day."

That was not what Evie was hoping she would say. She had to stop her from leaving. "Excuse me but . . . I'm new here and . . . well, correct me if I'm wrong, but you looked as though you didn't want to go inside the Infirmary earlier this morning." She moved a little closer towards her, biting the bullet—like she was occasionally able to do. "What's going on here?"

The girl frowned, almost perplexed herself. "You're ah . . . you're wondering? What's going *on*?"

Evie nodded earnestly.

The girl looked around again discreetly. "I knew deep down you looked different."

"Different?"

"When did you get here?"

Evie shrugged. "About a day or so ago . . . I think. It's hard to figure out."

"You want to know what's going on here?"

Evie nodded again. "Yes, very badly. And how I can get out of here!"

"Shhh!" said the girl aggressively. "We can't talk here, by no means." Then she let out a big, exaggerated laugh, tossed her head back and then patted Evie on the shoulder with one hand. She then spoke noticeably louder. "You must come and have lunch with me. I have a *beautiful* apartment. I'll help you settle in. I'll tell you about all the hot spots and in no time, you'll feel like you belong!"

A performance, it was obvious to Evie. But why? Who was she performing to? Next, she linked arms with Evie and walked down the road in a care-free way, looking straight ahead and finding things to giggle at.

"Your second question, I can't answer right at this moment," she said once they had gone for a short walk and were now inside the American girl's spacious apartment. "But I can have a good crack at your first one."

"Why couldn't we talk in the street?" asked Evie, feeling a bit put out by a tiring walk up-hill.

The girl replied like it was obvious. "Because you never know who might be listening of course!" As she spoke in a half-whisper, she was still looking around cautiously, darting from window to window, peering out of them quickly with a worried expression. "It's dangerous to talk at all," she said, coming back into the middle of the room, seeming satisfied that no one was going to overhear them.

"Why? Who is it we're afraid of?"

"Everyone. *Any*one. You can't trust a soul."

"Why not?" she asked wide-eyed.

"Look we haven't got much time. We've probably already been detected and there'll be people on our tail. So can you just keep your mouth shut and listen."

Evie suddenly decided that perhaps *this girl* was who she should be afraid of.

". . . Now where was I?"

". . . You can answer my first question?"

"Oh yeah. What's going on here . . . well . . . you were probably wondering why I was being dragged against my will into the Infirmary."

Evie just nodded, timidly.

"On my way in, I spotted you and I guessed straight away. That's happened to you too, right?"

Evie shook her head.

"But . . . you were coming out of the Infirmary. You were looking at me like . . ."

"Well, at least . . . I wasn't dragged in there. But I suppose it was against my will. I was out to it."

"Oh," she replied very knowingly. "Well when you've been here as long as I have and you don't conform to their ways, they don't bother keeping so many secrets from you anymore."

"What kind of secrets?"

"The great secret. That this place is a prison. Not a getaway luxury resort or an oversized retirement village as most people believe it to be. You tried to escape, yeah?"

"Well . . . I suppose I did when I think about it. I just wanted to go for a walk and see how far this place went on for. I came to a certain point and then I couldn't walk any further."

"Useless. Nobody will ever just *walk* out of here. There's like an invisible bubble encircling the Sanctuary. Impossible to penetrate. If you tried doing that, they'll say you tried to escape—and I don't blame you. But it's useless. How do I know? Because for as many weeks as I've been here, that's how many times I've tried to escape.

Any plan you could think of—I've tried it. I've tried going straight through, I've tried going up and over, I've tried going down and under. But every time, I've failed. Whenever you get close—as soon as you finally feel some kind of hope that you might *just* make it . . . there come the guys in black."

"I remember guys in black," Evie said, casting her fuzzy memory back to last night.

"All they do is bring you back to the Infirmary. For you and other newcomers, they knock you out with a . . . special kind of patch thing that goes on your arm. With me, they don't bother all the time, because I know what goes on."

"But all the bystanders . . . ?"

"Oh they're not bothered. They're all either patched themselves or they're just content to stay out of it and stay happy."

"Don't they . . . *patch* you?"

"Oh I've been patched before. I've had my gaa gaa moments. But it's a matter of staying wise and staying alert."

"And what about this not talking in the street stuff? Are there undercover cops on the street or something?"

"A1's men. Very possibly, but it's not only that. There's surveillance in public places. Who knows where they watch from, but I know they do."

"That's horrible."

"You're telling *me*."

"So this A1 dude, he's the guy who spoke to me yesterday. He seemed nice. Except he was a little creepy."

"If he seemed so nice, what made you think he was creepy? You can't be nice *and* creepy can you?"

"The way he sort of 'popped' in and out. I look around and he's there. And I look away and then back again and he's gone."

"He's like that. He doesn't have magic powers or anything, but he thinks it makes him look enigmatic."

"Enig . . . ?"

"Er, mysterious . . . unfathomable."

"Well he is that."

"Yeah, well just remember he's the bad guy in all of this."

"Hang on a minute. How do I know *you're* not the bad guy in all this?" Evie plucked up the courage to say. "You just said how you can't trust anyone. Why are you trusting me? And why should I trust you? I don't even know your name yet."

She looked sad. "I feel like I don't have a name anymore. 7B12 is my 'name' here. Sorry I didn't introduce myself properly. It's just that a name doesn't seem to mean anything here." Her face seemed to soften and in her eyes, Evie detected a sort of longing suddenly.

7B12 looked around again, as if checking whether anyone could be listening again. Then she looked real earnestly at Evie—right into her eyes and then said in a more hushed voice. "My name's Laura." Then she added, "And I think I trust you because . . . well, when I caught a glimpse of you outside the Infirmary, I just *knew* you were different. I've come across many undercover guys—trying to make me trust them. But you're nothing like them." She laughed pitifully at herself, "But you're standing there thinking that I could be saying all this to try and get you to trust me. I could be lying. Everything I'm saying could just be a script—handed to me by A1.

All I can say is that it's not. That I'm being truthful. That I'm *on your side*."

"I suppose it could be the other way around," replied Evie. "You don't know me from a bar of soap. *I* could be trying to trick *you*."

"I'd thought of that. But if we're going to get anywhere, I reckon we just take a giant leap of faith and trust each other. Despite what I said earlier."

"Well you have an honest face."

"D14, you can't be a successful double agent with a *dishonest* face can you?"

Evie didn't know what to do. She had no ideas of how to get out of this place by herself. She did need somebody. But what if Laura turned out to be a liar?

She made a decision. What did she have to lose? If she fell into a trap, then she'd be no worse off than she was now—stuck and clueless.

She looked up at Laura in the face and gave a little smile. "My name's Evie."

"I assume you know where we're going," Paulo said to Asher, rather impatiently.

"Paulo," said the Captain, "don't be rude."

"Well it almost feels like we've gone around in a circle."

The group had set off on their mission and had come back to the lush, wide open, green countryside.

"This is where we started," he continued.

"Which is *also* where we saw Evie disappear, remember?"

"But surely we would have saved so much time, if we'd have just stayed around here . . ."

"Hush," said Elsa. "You need to place more trust in Asher. Has he not fed you and sheltered you so far?"

This closed Paulo's mouth. You mustn't blame him though. He was just feeling anxious for Evelyn. People on Serothia had a great deal of concern for other people, no matter who they are. That's why it's such a friendly place.

"This is the place," said Asher. "This is where we believe there is evidence for the Sanctuary."

Believe there is evidence . . . what a curious sentence, thought the Captain. "Er, why can't we see it?" he asked.

"We think that it's in another dimension to this one. In the same place, but in its own . . ." Asher seemed to be searching for an appropriate word.

"Dimension?"

He nodded, "Yes."

"Interesting." The Captain put his hands in his pockets and walked around the place. He put on his glasses in a flicker of hope that something might show up through the lens. But nothing did of course. When he turned around and kept pacing the area (goodness knows what he was doing—looking for vibes, Paulo wondered), he spotted the Train quite a distance off through the glasses—still standing proudly at the top of a hillside. He looked at it for a while, narrowed his eyes and then said, "I wonder . . ."

Laura smiled back. "It's a pleasure to meet you Evie. But we'll have to be D14 and 7B12 most of the time."

"Why *is* that? What's wrong with people having their proper names?"

Laura shrugged. "Form of control I suppose. And this way, we can all be catalogued, indexed and monitored.

This whole thing's a conspiracy. I keep thinking *what's it all for?* And I still haven't gotten to the bottom of that one. I keep expecting some awful thing to happen. For us to be released one by one unto to a terrifying monster for A1's entertainment or, I don't know, be used as slave workers for some sinister, evil project. But nope. Nothing happens. Nothing *ever* happens. We're just . . . kept. It's as if . . ." Laura broke off suddenly, and there was silence for a few seconds while her face changed to dread.

"What is it?"

"Shhh." Laura spoke in a whisper that was hardly even audible. "Don't say another word." She was looking down at the skirting board♣ near the front door of her apartment.

Evie followed her eye line and saw a power point mounted on the wall. For a second she wondered what the problem could possibly be. But then she noticed a tiny silver piece of metal resting on top of the power point. "What is it?" she asked.

"I've been so stupid," Laura said, as she stepped over towards it. Then she did something strange. She gathered some force, lifted her right leg and then her foot came slamming down on the piece of metal as if she was squashing a spider. Then, she bent over and picked the (now even tinier) thing up, examined it, observed it was now broken and said to Evie regretfully, holding it up in the air. "We're in trouble . . . They know."

♣   The bit that joins the wall to the floor.

Chapter Seven

Déjà Vu

The Captain had been rustling around in his Train for at least ten minutes, searching all the surfaces, looking under the floor, fossicking through drawers. Paulo had asked what he was looking for, but it had been no use. He just gave a non-specific, almost unintelligible reply. So he decided to wait outside the Train and watch Asher and his crew mill about a little distance off, down the hill. Asher always seemed to be closest to Jon and Pintz and they were often found in a smaller group, chatting a few yards off from the others. Those others seemed to be much more like followers. They wouldn't know what to do apart from Asher.

Suddenly, the Captain emerged from the Train, saying, "Ta daa!" and holding up what looked like a magnifying glass. His pockets also seemed to be noticeably bulkier. He strode over to Paulo and said with a smile, "I haven't used this in years! I don't know why I kept forgetting about it, it's been very useful to me on occasions in the past . . . and in the future come to think of it."

"A magnifying glass?" As Paulo said it, he got the opportunity to see it a bit closer up, and he now noticed that it was quite a chunky magnifying glass—particularly the handle. It had buttons and switches on it!

"Correction," said the Captain, whilst walking down the hill, with Paulo following close beside him. "It's a Dimensionally Versatile Ocular Portal Lens."

Even though this sounded to Paulo yet again like one of the Captain's over-complicatedly-named bizarre gadgets, he did understand some of the individual words. "Dimensionally . . . versatile . . . do you mean, you'll be able to see things that are in a different dimension?!"

"Emphasis on *might*. I can't always tune in the right dimension." He was twiddling a knob on the handle—both clockwise and anticlockwise. "I'm setting its dials so that it can show me this very spot exactly one hour in the past." He then held it up in front of his face and looked at Paulo. For Paulo, the Captain's bulging pupil and speckled blue iris filled the circumference of the glass. From the Captain's point of view, everything was the same, except Paulo was not standing in front of him.

"Good, it's working," he said, as they were just approaching the others at the bottom of the hill. "Now I've just got to get it on the right setting," he then muttered to himself.

"Captain, are we to stand around all day *waiting* for a passage into the Sanctuary to *open up* for us?" Asher said to the Captain sarcastically.

The Captain was taken aback and he answered literally. "I never made that suggestion."

Pintz spoke next. "Asher means, you're not filling him with confidence. We've been here ten minutes, and you've done nothing."

"Nothing?" The Captain seemed quite offended. He turned to Paulo and said quietly—just to him, "They're an impatient lot aren't they."

"Yes but, Captain," he replied in a hushed voice, "Do you know what dimension the place is in, in order to see it in your . . . Dimensionally . . . your erm . . . your magnifying glass?"

"No. So I'm just going to have to try all the frequencies. And *they're* going to have to be patient."

From then on, Paulo seemed to become the Captain's sort of messenger man—transmitting the Captain's explanations to Asher's mob in slightly more understandable words.

"The Captain has some tools that he's going to experiment with to try and locate the Sanctuary."

The Captain kept on twiddling the knob on the handle and then he pressed a button.

"What's he doing?" asked Marnya, obviously not yet impressed by anything the Captain had done so far.

Asher was more interested than unimpressed. "I've never seen anything like it."

He would turn the knob and then look through the glass, then press a few buttons and then look through the glass again. Sometimes he would walk around with it, and then stoop over, looking through it. He looked just like Sherlock Holmes looking for clues, minus the hat.

After a while, he started to become frustrated—tutting a lot and muttering to himself. "It's going to be the last one I try, I just *know* it."

"What's supposed to happen?" Pintz asked Paulo.

"I think he can *see* different dimensions through it."

Pintz looked curiously at Asher.

Paulo then whispered to the Captain, "Just how many dimensions are there to sort through?"

"Well, there's a theory that they're endless."

Paulo's eyes widened. "You mean *infinite?*"

"Yes."

"That's hard to fathom. How do you expect to find the right one?"

"I don't really. But it's worth a try." He gave Paulo an optimistic grin, and as he looked up to do the grin, it rapidly turned into a frown. He muttered a word—a name, that Paulo wasn't expecting. "Evelyn."

"Where?!"

"No, sorry, not Evelyn herself. That chap over there. Ross."

"Roscoe."

"That's the guy."

Paulo paused for a moment. "Well I'm sorry, I don't see the connection. Even someone going blind could see that he doesn't bare the slightest resemblance to Evie at all!"

"That's exactly how Evelyn was acting just before she disappeared." He quickly began walking toward Roscoe who had wandered a little way from the group down the hill.

Asher knew something was wrong when the Captain flew past him with a serious, urgent expression. "What is it, Captain? Found a way of getting in?"

"Somebody help me to *wake Roscoe up!*" he shouted.

"What's he talking about?" said Elsa.

"Roscoe!" called the Captain.

"This place is beautiful!" said Roscoe in reply.

"Roscoe! Come back!"

It was too late. Suddenly, there was a blinding light which engulfed Roscoe and the Captain could get no further towards him. The others behind him were cowering from the light, and then blocking their ears from the sound.

When it fell quiet again—when they could finally look up to see what had happened, there was no trace of Roscoe.

The Captain closed his eyes and drooped his head, angry at himself for not being able to stop it.

All Evie knew, was that she had to follow Laura. They were soon out the door and running along the hilly lane that wound around behind Laura's apartment building.

She was already out of breath and tried to ask, "Where are we going?"

"Don't know yet. But we can't stay at my place. We'll just run! It'll at least confuse them for a while. In this place, there's a general rule if you ever want to escape. Always confuse the enemy!"

What if Laura was the enemy? Evie couldn't help thinking. This girl could be leading her straight into a trap!

Laura suddenly came to a stop. They had not only wound back from the apartments, but also *up* and so they almost had an aerial view of where they had come from. There were lots of trees growing up here and Laura was watching the road to her apartment building from behind one of them.

"Get behind that tree, Evie! Do you want them to see you?"

"Where *are* they?"

"Nowhere to be seen yet. But they'll come, trust me."

There was that word again—*trust.* Evie's head was all in a spin.

"My apartment was bugged. They must have got there before us and planted a microphone there. I told you it was unsafe to talk in the street. They suspected ever since we laid eyes on each other."

Just as Evie was getting her breath back, she saw movement down by the apartments. Four men in black were marching straight for Laura's front door.

"There they are!" Evie whispered and turned to run.

"Don't move! Not yet," said Laura. "We'll wait 'till they've gone inside."

They watched in silence, until the men disappeared around a corner.

"That's our cue," Laura said, and she turned and ran further up the hill, deeper into the trees. Evie's thighs were killing from the climb. Her blood was running hot—heart pumping fast, yet her skin was cold from the morning air. The trees got thicker and thicker and the hillside now looked like a very neat forest—all the trees in dead straight rows and columns. They'd come over the crest of the hill and were now looking down over the other side where the trees were even denser. So thick that they couldn't see the ground beneath them.

Where to now?"

"Through the forest," Laura said. "Probably the safest place is the forest. They don't have surveillance in the forest."

"The trees aren't bugged are they?"

Laura smiled. "Not to my knowledge. Come on, let's get a move on."

Evie pushed past the pain in her legs. But this was the least of her worries. As they ran through all the trees, branches would slap into their chests and past their cheeks and the long damp grass would tug at their ankles. Evie kept looking behind her. There didn't seem to be any sign of anyone following them. But Laura didn't stop running, and she never wasted precious energy to look back.

They were getting further and further very quickly—to the point where Evie would never be able to find her way back to 'her home' or to the Square by herself. She took another quick glance behind her. Still nothing. But this time, she tripped over an above-ground tree root and let out a little yelp of surprise. Laura stopped, turned back to help her up, but a sound—unnatural to the forest made them both look up at each other before Evie was back on her feet. It was the sound of a motor intruding the peace of the forest.

Laura had a look of dread on her face. "They're on their motor bikes."

"Does that mean we've lost?"

"It means we've gotta run faster. Come on."

They ran side by side, until Laura took a sharp turn to the right. Evie turned quickly to follow her, but the sound of the bike seemed to come from that direction now. She turned back to the left, but could tell that there was actually a second bike—and they had separated to come rounding up on both sides.

"Laura!" she cried out.

The motors were getting louder every second. Evie even felt the vibration of the engines through the ground, off the trees. She caught a glimpse of Laura suddenly—on lower ground a little way off. But she gasped out loud when she saw a motor bike and its rider approaching her fast from behind. "Laura!!" she yelled out again to try and warn her.

The rider skidded around, pivoting on the bike's front wheel, thrusting a whirl of fallen leaves into the air. He landed right in front of Laura, and before she had a chance to change direction, the man in black was off his bike and coming towards her.

Evie realised she was on her own. What did Laura say? The forest. Head for the forest—it's the safest place. Evie looked around desperately . . . she was *in* the forest! Where was the *next* safest place?

She decided to just keep on running, because she could still hear the motor of the second bike, getting nearer and nearer. Perhaps there was deeper forest still yet to come—more places to hide.

As she was running, she couldn't determine which direction the motor bike was coming from. The sound seemed to bounce off the trees and trick her all the time. She kept turning her head to see if she could see anything. On one occasion she had been looking behind her and when she looked ahead again to see where she was going . . .

The man on the motor bike was riding towards her head-on. When she changed direction, the expert pursuer outsmarted her and cut her line of escape off before she could blink. She changed direction quickly again, but this time, her foot slid on the damp mushy leaves under foot and she landed with a heavy thud on her stomach in the dirt. She felt strong hands grabbing her under the arms and yanking her off the ground.* She struggled for a while to get free, but it was no use. The

---

* So much for school helping you out in life situations. She was reminded of P.E. lessons and the beep test—having to change direction like that very quickly. Well, it never did her any good then, and it certainly didn't do her any good now.

man's fingers were like metal clamps screwed in on their tightest setting. Soon, she was with Laura again, and the two of them were taken all the way back on foot to the Infirmary.

Chapter Eight

Bermuda

"What happened?" asked Marnya, gob smacked by the disappearance of Roscoe.

"That's *exactly* what happened to my friend," the Captain told them. Then he asked Asher, "Any ideas?"

"No, I've never seen that before. There's obviously some strange force if you enter into a particular zone."

"He said '*this place is beautiful*'. Evelyn said things like that. There could be some hypnotising properties in the atmosphere, or . . . or in the grass and these flowers growing here and there." A new energy seemed to overtake the Captain, as he got out a couple of different tools from his pocket and knelt down on the ground.

Paulo came over to him and bent over to speak, "What about the Dimensionally Versatile Ocular Portal Lens? Have you gotten it to work?"

"It seems to react to one particular dimension, but I still can't see anything through it. As if someone's deliberately trying to keep the Sanctuary hidden using another equally clever tool."

"So, what are you thinking now?"

"I think we've got to get in there fast."

"Well I hate to state the obvious but . . . what about the Train?"

"Yes. Don't think that it hasn't crossed my mind," he said, picking some grass out of the ground and examining it. "There are dangers in that."

"What dangers?"

"Same dangers there are if we were to get in by ourselves. Will it ever be able to come out again?"

"You mean it could get stuck there?"

"Yes. Just like we could get stuck there. Just like Evie's gotten stuck there."

"And now Roscoe."

"Or, there could be a possibility of the Train being confiscated. By the way Asher talks, it sounds like it's that kind of place."

The others had joined them now to check on the Captain's progress.

"What do you think, Captain?" said Asher. "Can we get in or what?"

"It's feasible. But one of the most efficient ways I can think of and probably the quickest is to get in the same way as Evelyn and Roscoe did. Get ourselves deliberately intoxicated by whatever is in the air round here."

"That's a terrible idea, Captain."

"Is it?"

"Yes," Jon continued. "Go in that way and you're immediately under their radar. We'll all be captured and probably put straight into the Infirmary."

"That sounds nasty," said Paulo. "What's that?"

"It's like a recuperating and treating clinic—like a hospital. But they do all sorts of sinister things in there. And we certainly won't be any use from in there."

"Right," said the Captain, walking with a purpose further down the hill to where Roscoe disappeared from.

Paulo started to follow.

"No Paulo, you'd better stay here."

"Captain, you can try all you like but I'm staying with you. Don't you remember rule number one?"

"What rule?"

"The rule you set for me. I'm to stay with you. And I'm not accustomed to breaking rules."

"Oh yes . . . blasted rules. Okay then, come on."

"What are you doing, Captain?" asked Pintz.

"Stay back!" he called. "We're entering very beautiful ground!"

Paulo looked at him oddly.

The Captain paused and then shook his head. "I mean very *dangerous* ground."

"Were you joking then, Captain?"

He looked a little bemused. "Er . . ." he hesitated. "Er . . . yes." Then he fixed his eyes onto something that apparently interested him. "Look at that."

"What? Have you found a clue?"

The Captain knelt over to pick it up. Paulo frowned suspiciously when he saw, that it was a wild flower.

"Isn't that gorgeous! So unusual." Then he straightened up with it in his hand and looked around. "What a perfect place for a picnic or something." He smiled, looking up to the clouds.

"Oh no you don't!" Paulo said, shaking the Captain's arm. He then pulled the Captain's face back down and looked him in the eye. "Captain!"

He blinked a few times. "Sorry? What is it?"

"We're not here to enjoy the wildlife! You're supposed to be examining the hypnotic effects of this area!"

He blinked again and rubbed his eyes. Then his face showed utter gratitude and he patted Paulo on the shoulder. "Yes of course. Thank you." He looked up to where the others were, looking on. "I think this is far too dangerous. I'll have to think of something else."

He wearily walked passed Paulo and back up the hill. He explained to Asher and the rest of the group what had happened and told them not to cross a certain point on the hillside.

"What I think we could do is try and walk around the circumference of the Sanctuary. We know it's around here somewhere. It's definitely in another dimension, but it has some kind of presence still in this dimension. Any idea how big it is?"

They all shook their heads. But the Captain got the idea that they were all thinking it was pretty large, and that none of them had ever got the chance to grasp just how far reaching the place was.

"Well, we'll just keep walking along here, I'll try and get some readings on my instrument here, and we'll try and map out its walls."

"Sounds very time consuming," said Marnya.

"It is, but it's the only way I can think of making a start."

"Right," said Asher. "Well we'll set off then . . . just a minute . . ."

"What?"

"Where's your friend got to?"

"Evelyn? Well, I think she's in the Sanctuary. I told you didn't I? Or rather, you told me."

"No no no, you're other friend—Paulo."

The Captain quickly looked around, and he wasn't by his side, as he had just promised confidently that he would be.

"There!" cried Marnya.

They all looked. He was down the hill a bit, taking in huge deep breaths of the fresh clean air of the countryside, dancing around in its beauty. He'd never actually left the spot where he and the Captain were talking just a minute ago.

"Paulo! No!"

And it happened again, to the Captain's horror. The flash of light. The screeching sound. All over in a matter of seconds. Their group of eight, was now down to six. And the Captain felt completely responsible.

The giant ominous walls of the Infirmary grew larger and larger as Evie and Laura were led closer to them. The very tops of them seemed to leer down at the girls as though the whole thing was a cruel, nonsensical joke. Laura pictured those same old white plastered walls that she would soon be between and Evie wondered what horrors awaited them. More useless interrogation . . . more attempts to convince her that she hated her life. Laura, on the other hand, knew the horrors. And they were all just routine for her now.

The big doors opened and they were hustled inside. They were taken down a couple of corridors together, but at the end of one of them, Laura was taken to the left, and Evie was taken to the right. Evie tried to resist their force, but there wasn't a thing she could do about it. She had finally found a friend—or at least someone who could help her understand the place—and now she was being separated from her. She didn't fancy being on her own again.

Laura tried to yell out, "Stay alert! Don't let them . . ." The rest was muffled because a gloved hand came over her mouth.

Evie was pushed along several more corridors until she'd lost all sense of direction. Next thing, she was in a room. That same room again, with 'Mark' and his clipboard.

"Why did you run?" he asked after she was seated.

"Because someone was listening in to a private conversation I was having I suppose."

"Why did you run to the forest? Were you trying to escape?"

"No. But if that happened, I wouldn't have been disappointed."

"Why did you try to escape?"

"I just said I didn't . . ."

"Why did you seek the Sanctuary?"

"I didn't. I was *brought* here against . . ."

"What is your affiliation with 7B12?"

"I don't know what affiliation means."

"Why were you conversing with 7B12?"

"Because I felt like it."

It went on. Evie was never sure of what the right thing to say would be. The only thing she had to go on was, 'stay alert!' What did that mean, anyway? She just decided to take a leaf out of Laura's book and *not* cooperate. Being in the company of that strong-willed girl, caused her to come out of her shell a bit more than usual. She was suddenly bolder and less concerned with the terrible fear she was still feeling and used it more for adrenalin.

She would never conform to what they wanted her to become. She would never admit that she came here by choice . . .

She hoped she was doing the right thing.

"Right," said the Captain, looking at the readings from his magnifying glass again. "We'll just have to go in the easy way then."

"You mean the *hard* way," said Asher.

"No I mean the easy way."

Asher looked astounded and impatient. "What do you mean the *easy* way?!"

"It could very well be the hard way at the same time. But we need to find Evelyn and Paulo fast."

"And Roscoe," said Elsa.

"And Roscoe. For all we know, they could be in terrible danger and I don't fancy spending hours and hours, possibly days to find out. If you'll all come this way," the Captain said, leading the group reluctantly up the hill and towards the Train.

When Paulo managed to get his eyes open, all he could see was a high ceiling. He blinked a few times to get his vision into focus, and staring down at him was a white, buzzing florescent light. He felt woozy, but he thought that he just might be able to sit up to try and see where he was. He could see that he was in a white hospital bed, with white sheets and a white blanket.

He looked around the eerily silent room. It was large—T-shaped. Walls wood-paneled half way up, and the top half painted white. Ugly yellow and orange curtains. His bed was one of many, lined up along the walls, parallel with each other. His bed was the only one occupied.

"And how are we feeling, C36? All rested and ready to begin the day?"

". . . Pardon?"

"And what a lovely day it is, too."

He tried standing up out of bed.

"Can you manage?" A nursey-looking woman approached him and went to help him up from under the arms, but he shrugged her off.

"Yes, I can manage I think." He stood up alright, but he was a bit wobbly. "Where am I?"

"Don't worry yourself about it. You're in safe hands now. You'll be well taken care of."

"Yes, but *where am I?*"

"The Infirmary," she replied as if it was a silly question. "Come along and let me take you to the Recovery Room."

"Where's Roscoe?"

"Roscoe? I don't know what a Roscoe is, I'm sorry. Just come along with me. You'll feel better in an hour or so."

"He must be here!"

Paulo was causing quite a scene by this time, and another woman came through and met with the first one.

"Anything wrong 317?"

"This one appears to be having delusions."

"Well take him to the Recovery Room. Give it an hour. And if he continues in that way . . . you know what to do."

"Yes, A12." Then the woman (317) spoke to Paulo and the older woman left briskly. "Come on C36, all your questions will be answered if you come this way."

Paulo reluctantly moved towards her and followed her out of the room with the beds and through a few corridors, until they came to a door that the woman opened.

Paulo assumed he was supposed to go inside, but he didn't straight away. "What do you mean by calling me C36? What's that all about?"

"Everything will be explained to you," she replied in a cool, calm voice, and then invited him to enter the room.

He did, reluctantly and hesitantly, and as soon as he was over the threshold, the door was closed behind him.

And what a strange room it was, full of strange people. Apparently his entering the room, affected none of them. Not one of them flinched an eyeball. They all just kept on doing what they were doing. Some were on the floor playing with children's toys, a couple were reading, all squished up in a corner keeping to themselves and there were some just sitting in chairs, just staring. And that irritating, stifling music . . .

Suddenly, he stopped dead-still. His heart raced and he went clammy all over with shock. In one of those chairs—staring straight ahead, watching the tiny particles of dust in the air . . . was Evelyn.

Paulo raced over to her, exclaiming her name . . . but she didn't notice him. Her face was blank. He touched her on the arm and spoke softly to her. "Evie? It's so good to see you. What is this place?"

Her eyes moved from staring straight ahead, to meet his eyes. Then she turned her head to face him. But deep in her eyes, there was no change of expression. She could see him perfectly well, but Paulo's heart sank when he realised she did not recognise him. She blinked a few times, gave an empty, care-free smile and then stared straight ahead again.

Paulo was in despair just looking at her. "Oh Evie," he whispered. "What have they done to you?"

Chapter Nine

Admit Six—The Sanctuary

Paulo didn't know what to do, but his mere reaction, was to get up and start pounding on the door of the Recovery Room to hopefully get the attention of one of those nurses. He had no luck straight away, but he kept on persisting. He half expected to be told off by the occupants of the room for disturbing their peace and quiet, but like before, no one really bothered. They looked around a bit, observing a few seconds of the commotion but that was it. Paulo pounded on the door until his fists hurt, and called out through the door until he got sick of his own voice.

Finally, somebody came. It was the older matronly looking woman from before who was referred to as A12. She looked stern and Paulo had to make a conscious effort not to be frightened of her.

She said very calmly, looking down her nose at him. "What is all this noise about?"

Paulo swallowed. "I want to know what's happened to my friend Evie in here. She's not herself. She doesn't know who I am!"

"I know no person of that name." She went to close the door on him again, but he persisted.

"You must know her, she's right here!" And he pointed to her.

"That is D14. And you mustn't be alarmed. It is only an initial short term side-effect of her treatment. It's all part of the process to happy living here in the Sanctuary."

"What *treatment?* It's not natural!"

"It's perfectly natural. She'll be as right as rain in an hour or so."

Paulo frowned. He still wasn't satisfied. "Well can I at least take her out of this place?" Paulo thought that being in this room, around all these weird people, was only making things worse for Evie.

A12 seemed to consider his request for a short moment, and then replied, "Very well. But you'll have to be discharged yourself."

"How long will that take?"

"If you're not still feeling woozy from sleep, you can go to the front check-in station to be signed out. But the people there will need written permission from me first."

That all happened. But somehow, Paulo was never back with Evie. He was given their word that she would also be released and taken back to her home, but Paulo was expecting to stay with her. He was wrong. There was a big bothersome procession organised to put him into a vehicle and sent to his own new home. He kept getting called C36, which was really getting on his nerves, and he never seemed to get a chance to ask anyone the questions he wanted to ask.

He was soon hustled out of the vehicle and being pointed to a door, which was one of several, all evenly spaced out along the front of a long building. The door he was shown to had the number C36 in silver plating on it. They left him there to settle in on his own. When he opened the door, he was utterly astounded to see an exact copy of his very own compact living quarters near the Satellite Training Complex back on Serothia.

"What a curious little vehicle," said Asher as he and those who remained of his group entered the Train's engine room. "Clever way of not being seen."

"What, being invisible? Yes, I dare say it is," the Captain replied, with a slight touch of sarcasm. He cringed afterwards though; he was trying to give up sarcasm.

"What exactly do you plan to do from in here, Captain?" asked Jon.

"From in *here*," the Captain replied, "I plan to get in *there*. *The Sanctuary*. Hold that for me will you, please." It was his Dimensionally Versatile Ocular Portal Lens that he wanted Jon to hold, so that he could use both his hands to work the controls of the Train.

He copied combinations of numbers from the readings on the lens and entered them into a computerised panel on the middle console of the Train.

"You mean this thing can hop between dimensions?" Jon asked.

"On my lucky days," he replied, not helping at all to gain the group's confidence. "Hold it still! If I get just one of these numbers wrong, we could end up on the moon . . . of a distant planet . . . in another universe . . . 200 years in the future."

That kept them all quiet.

Asher sighed. "Are you *sure* you can get us into the Sanctuary?"

"I told you. If it's a lucky day. Although I'd prefer not to rely on luck. Would you mind if we all joined hands for a minute? . . . No? Okay, can I just say a quick prayer myself then?"

"A quick prayer? What's the man talking about?" asked Pintz.

"Never mind. Already done it. Let's go!" He pulled a lever and suddenly the Train whirred into action. The passengers had to hang on tight while they heard a deep chuffing and puffing sound coming from the very core of the Train.

> ***Chuff*** *choofety chuff, choofety **chuff** choofety bang!*
> *Choofety **chuff** choofety chuff, choofety **chuff** choofety bang!*

The sound grew louder than usual and the ride was bumpier than usual and the Captain had to shovel in more Carnane fuel* than usual. He figured this was a good sign, because anybody knows that the power needed to hop through dimensions is much greater than what's needed to simply hop through normal space.

There was a *DING* from a control panel against the wall.

"Well, the water's nice and hot if anybody fancies a cup of tea," said the Captain, after he'd finished shovelling in the fuel.

"Surprisingly, nobody feels like a cup of tea just at the moment, *Captain*," said Jon, his own temper beginning to boil along with the water.

The Captain shrugged, "Suit yourself."

It turned out to be lucky no one decided to have a cup of tea anyway because the Train ride suddenly got a

---

* A special type of fuel that the Train needs to be able to go. It looks like glowing lumps of coal.

good deal bumpier. The passengers were jolted from side to side—kind of like you are in an ordinary train but with a bit more severity. The Captain was hanging onto the control deck with one hand, and with the other, he was manipulating controls in order to try and stabilise the Train.

"Is this normal, Captain?" asked Pintz.

"Perfectly! . . . I think. Just have to materialise," which in this case was going to be a very fiddly business, so the Captain demanded silence then, so that he could concentrate.

Paulo spent no time at all relaxing in his apartment (like they probably wanted him to). The moment he got there, he was straight out again—in search of Evie. On his way past the door, he saw the letter and numbers 'C36' and remembered that that's what they kept calling him. *What did they call Evie?* Paulo tried to remember. He remembered it was a 14 because it matched her age.* But there was a letter in front. *A? . . . no. B? . . . no. C? . . . no. D? . . . no. E? . . . YES! It was D! 'D14'.*

Paulo got a rush of excitement but then his heart sank again very quickly. How was he supposed to find a house or apartment or whatever it was, numbered D14? He didn't have a street directory. He didn't even know how big the Sanctuary was. He still couldn't believe how he could have gotten trapped in here—even after he'd learnt how it happened, how Evie got trapped in the first place.

He noticed all the doors along the same wall as his, had 'C-something' on it. He figured they must be

---

*   Purely coincidental.

organised by the letters. This was 'C' area, and not far away might be the 'D' area!

He decided to go for a brisk walk.

It wasn't too long before he got a brief idea of how the housing worked. It was very organised as he'd hoped, and the 'D' area wasn't too far away from the 'C' area. Although being organised, parts of it didn't look very logical. There were roads where the houses along it looked very different from each other. Usually, houses next door to each other look quite similar because they are built around the same time frame or are of the same value. But the roads of houses here were quite curious. There'd be an ultra modern looking house right next door to a huge old stone building with ivy creeping along its walls. Big triple story mansions right next door to flat, cheap looking units. It even looked like there were houses from completely different cultures built right next to each other. They were not just all lined up along the road either. Some would be back away from the road with a windy overgrown pathway leading up to the front door, and some would be standing sideways to the road. It basically looked like someone had picked the odd house from different suburbs and different countries all over the world, collected them all and placed them together in one neighbourhood.

When he finally found the number 'D14' on a white box attached to the fence, he rushed up to a house that had one floor and a front yard that had leaves from the trees all over it. It looked strange to Paulo because he wasn't from Earth, but to you and me, it would have looked like a very average, middle-class house. It was tucked away on its own—away from its closest neighbours—and there was a light on inside.

He sped up to the front door and knocked urgently. The door was answered to him, and Evie greeted him with a smile. He was so relieved to see her, but she didn't act as he had expected her to.

"Hello. How are you? Would you like to come in?" was what she said.

Paulo did enter, but he was looking at her curiously.

After she closed the door again, Paulo said hesitantly, "You *do* know who I am, don't you?"

"Of course I do," she said, smiling.

Paulo breathed a sigh of relief.

"You're C36. I saw you in the Recovery Room. And it's thanks to you that I'm out of there so I'm told."

". . . Yeah." (Then he whispered to her), "Obviously it's dangerous to talk or something, is it Evie? I've kind of gathered that the people in charge here are rather . . . controlling."

"People in charge? Controlling? What are you talking about? And what is . . . *Evie?*"

"Look, cut it out. What is this place? I know it's called the Sanctuary, but what goes on here? Why have we been pulled into it?"

"The Sanctuary is a place to . . . to breath I guess. To relax. Chill out. Be away from the hustle and bustle of life."

"Are you being serious?"

"Of course. I don't think I've ever felt happier than how I feel now."

"But Evie . . . !"

"My name is D14," she frowned. "What exactly do you want? I can get some milk and biscuits. Or do you want some tea? I can make some tea. Nothing like a good cup of tea, especially in such a calm and peaceful place like this."

She started walking towards her kitchen, but Paulo grabbed her by the shoulders and shook her.

"Snap out of it, Evie!" he yelled at her. "Wake up!!!"

Down by the beach at that moment, where lots of people were sunbathing and splashing in the water and dozing off on their fold out beach chairs, there was the sound of a steam train approaching—but nothing could be seen. It got louder and louder until abruptly, it stopped and it made a big huffy sigh with the bubbling and hissing of steam.

Then from out of nowhere on a rocky mound near the water, came a man dressed in baggy brown trousers, a shirt with a knitted vest over the top and a cap—baggy where it covered the head, but with a short, rounded brim at the front. He put on a big coat as he emerged from the Train. It was the Captain of course, followed slowly by Asher and four more astonished looking passengers. Jon, Pintz, Marnya and Elsa.

"Does this look familiar?" asked the Captain.

"Yes," replied Asher, with a kind of a dread in his voice. "This is the place. This is the Sanctuary alright. See how everybody's just sitting around doing nothing. None of them have even noticed us."

"Well let's just hope that everybody *else* doesn't notice us," said Elsa. "Like A1 and his army of puppets."

"Or the surveillance cameras," added Marnya, scanning the area cautiously.

"This does *look* like a lovely place to be," said the Captain, merely observing what he saw.

"Yeah, well don't be fooled," said Jon. "It's a prison. Like a straitjacket—you can't move."

"These people aren't acting very much like prisoners," said the Captain.

"That's because they're all controlled like marionette puppets. Even their feelings are controlled."

"What a pity. It looks like nothing could ever go wrong here."

"Think again," said Asher. "All A1 has to do is pull a string and . . ."

There was, at the moment, a loud scream near by. It sounded like it was coming from out in the water. They all looked immediately and saw that there was splashing and struggling in the water about a mile out. The Captain ran up to the water to get a closer look. It was a woman who was doing the screaming and kicking and shouting, and she was now being restrained by four men—all dressed in black wetsuits and once they had a good hold of her, they were swimming her back to the shore.

The Captain was this close to intervening, but it was Asher that stopped him. "We don't want to be noticed, remember Captain?"

Unfortunately nobody reminded Elsa of that fact. She recognised the woman in the water. She was someone Elsa had grown quite close to during her time in the Sanctuary. Someone who wasn't so lucky to get out as Elsa had been.

Before anyone could stop her, Elsa rushed out from behind the new arrivals and towards her friend. "Take your hands off her! Leave her alone!" For a moment, it looked like it was actually going to work. The men had loosened their grip on the woman being pulled in from the sea. But when the woman was released, she made no attempt to run away. Instead, she flopped to the ground and looked as though she was set for a very long sleep. Elsa tried to wake her friend when she arrived at her side, but the men took her away on a stretcher bed. And because Elsa had now exposed herself, she was also taken into custody and dragged away from the scene.

Now you would think that all this commotion would have surely drawn some attention from the sunbathers near by . . . wouldn't you?

If I said they ignored the commotion, it would imply that they had some kind of consciousness of it and chose not to pay it any attention. But they acted as though they weren't even aware of any of it going on nearby—as if the whole thing was so much of a regular occurrence, that they'd grown blind to it.

It was hard for the Captain to watch without jumping in to save the day. That's what he'd discovered he was good at. But he knew it would be futile. It was not yet time to be noticed.

"That's what would have happened to you, Captain," said Asher, "if you had have tried to save the woman. She was probably trying to swim out as far as she could to try and escape that way."

"Aren't you worried about Elsa?"

"We're saddened. Not worried, because we know exactly what will happen to her now."

"What?"

"She'll be taken to the Infirmary," Marnya explained tearfully, "and questioned, interrogated, possibly patched, and put into her own little house again with her own little routine. She'll be trapped like an animal in a cage again."

"What does it mean to be patched?"

"If you don't cooperate on too many occasions, they put a patch on your arm. It numbs you to the realities of this place, numbs you from your passion to fight back and be free—properly free."

"That's clever," said the Captain, almost with admiration, but then he added, "but *totally* cruel and unethical. They've got to be stopped!"

"That's the spirit!" said Asher. "That's what I've been waiting to hear."

"Just one thing before we continue our journey."

"What is it?"

"If that's what happens when you try and get out of this place, how did you all escape?"

"There's a different story for just about each and every one of us. Most of the time, a combination of coincidence, skill, know-how and imagination. I'll tell you more about it later. Shall I show you where A1 lives?"

"Yes," said the Captain. "Lead on." He felt dreadfully sorry for Elsa. Now they were down from eight to five. And how long would it be, until they were down to four?

Paulo had just finished yelling at Evie to try and get through to her, but all she did was smile vacantly back at him.

"How do you get out of here?" he said next. "There must be a way out!"

"Why would you want to leave?" Evie asked. "This is the coolest place ever! No school, no homework, no one telling us what to do . . ."

"But don't you see Evie? You're not meant to be here. This isn't your life. What about the Captain? What about your family back on Earth where you live?"

"Are you kidding? This place is way better!"

When Evie said that, Paulo knew that she wasn't well at all. He'd often heard her say in the past how much she cared for her family. Something had to be done. And Paulo was possibly the only person who could do it! He couldn't rely on the Captain and Asher and the others getting there to save the day. They may never even make it inside. Paulo decided he should try and get *out* so that he could tell the Captain just exactly what was going on and how Evie was behaving. The Captain would know what to do next.

"Well *I'm* going to get out," Paulo told Evie. "You stay right here."

And off he went. Evie was left in her house all alone, watching him disappear down the lane and heading for the square. She smiled to herself, knowing that he didn't stand a chance of getting out. She then slowly wandered over to her telephone, picked up the receiver and dialed a brief letter-and-number combination . . . A1.

"Yes D14?" a calm, male voice answered.

"You know C36? The newcomer?"

"Yes."

"Well he's going to try and escape. He just told me so. He's probably on his way through the square by now."

"Thank you very much, D14."

Chapter Ten

And Then There Was One

Determined . . . but clueless, Paulo was running non-stop. He really had no idea how he was going to try and get out. He wondered if it was as simple as getting out the same way he got in. It was the only idea he had so far. He decided to run as far out of the main part of the Sanctuary as he could. When he got that far, the ground sloped upwards and onto a large area of grassy hillside. It looked similar to the place where he was before he lost consciousness. So he kept on going. Maybe it was as simple as crossing a border. Or as easy as stepping through some kind of portal.

While he was running, he scanned the countryside with his eyes. There was no sign of anything, and after a long while of running around in the open, peaceful countryside, he started feeling ever so tired and feared he would not be able to go on. He'd been running as fast and as hard as he could and there was nothing left to do now but to stop and have a breather.

That is until he heard a sound that broke the silence a short distance from him back towards the centre of the Sanctuary—the sound of engines coming nearer and nearer. He suddenly found that he *could* go on. He discovered somehow that earlier, he hadn't been running nearly as fast as he could.

But suddenly something stopped him and his body flung backwards onto the grass and he lay on his back dumbfounded, staring up at the sky. He got up and tried to work out what he had run into. If it happened to you, you might say that it felt like colliding into the wall of a jumpy-castle.

Paulo was staggered to see in front of him—nothing. He lifted up his hands to try and feel for what might have been the barrier, but he didn't get a chance to find out. Only metres behind him, the engines had arrived. There were two cars; both with no roof. One had four men, all in black, jumping out of it with a stretcher bed, and the other had a man of middle age in the driver's seat, who was actually A1 himself. Next to him in the passenger's seat, sat Evie, looking almost amused.

"That is where A1 lives and works," Asher said to the Captain after the group had come around the last corner of their walk from the beach to the Sanctuary Square. "We can get to the bottom of all this if we can get in there we think."

The Captain was looking up at the big round building, which looked more like a factory than a home. Or something in between an office building and a factory. An office building, because there were no pipes on the roof with black smoke billowing up to the sky from them, and like a factory because the building had no windows. Just one large door at the front, in the middle at the bottom, which acted like a window as well because it was glass. There were neat, trimmed plants all around it, and coming out from the building towards you was a wide path that led up to the big door. There were plants growing on the flat roof right up the top—some of which were hanging over the edge and draping over the walls. The walls themselves were hardly picturesque though. They were made of smooth stone, painted grey—no texture at all; the same as the path leading up to the door. At the other end of the path (the one adjoining the road), there was a big, tall gate, keeping people out (unless they had a combination to the little keypad, which was mounted on the side). The gate went all the way around the building and it went a long way up—no one could ever have a hope of climbing it.

Asher pointed out the surveillance cameras to the Captain, which were built onto the high fencing at occasional intervals around the building and there was one mounted on a pole by the entrance of the building.

The Captain said finally, "Are you expecting me to find you all a way in?"

"No," replied Asher. "You have done your marvellous job at getting us back in here undetected . . ."

"As far as we know," said the worried Marnya.

"Now it's our turn," continued Asher. "I'm glad to say that at this point of the mission, we will be able to provide the resources and know-how to get us further."

"You see, during our time here," Pintz explained, "we managed to devise a way of getting into that building unnoticed. Those cameras have a blind spot. If we can all remain unseen by them, the rest is easy."

"What do you mean? We still have a twenty-foot tall gate to get past. Now unless you know the combination, I can't see how we're going to get through." The Captain knew that in one of his pockets he was bound to have a tool that could get them through somehow, but he didn't want to reveal all his secrets to Asher and his crew yet.

"But that's just *it*, Captain," said Jon. "We *do* know the combination. When Asher was brought here once for interrogation, he *saw the guard punch in the number!*"

"Wouldn't the guard have been more careful than that?"

"I was supposed to be unconscious at the time," said Asher. "But they clearly hadn't given me a strong enough patch."

"Asher," said Pintz.

"What is it?"

"I think I know how we're going to get inside. Look!"

They all looked at what Pintz was pointing at from behind the trees where they were. There was a man in white overalls with a trolley full of boxes, walking in the direction of the huge round building.

"Looks like a delivery," Asher said, hardly believing his eyes. "Right, we've got no time to lose. The blind spot we were talking about. That delivery man will pass it soon and when he does, we're going to be there waiting. We'll knock him out, I'll dress in his overalls and you lot can hop in the trolley. Covered in all those boxes, there's no way you'll be seen."

"Are you sure about this?" asked Marnya.

"Of course. It's too good a chance to pass up. And if we wait any longer, we won't have to pass it up—it'll pass itself up. Who's with me?"

Jon and Pintz agreed nervously and Marnya, exchanging glances with the Captain also anxiously agreed.

The Captain shrugged. "Well if anyone knows this place it's you fellows. We'll do it. I can't wait to finally have a word with this A1 chap."

"We'll walk up casually. I'll lead, and bring you all to the blind spot."

They walked casually across a small parkland which was part of the Sanctuary Square, across a cobblestone road, and then to a little niche between a curved edge of the big, tall gate and the sharp right-angle corner of a giant brick building next door.

There, they watched and waited for the delivery man to casually approach.

"What's this huge place next door?" the Captain asked quietly.

"That's the Infirmary. Right next door to A1. This part of town is where it all happens; it's the control centre if you like. The heart beat of the Sanctuary." He stopped talking. "Shhh, here he comes."

When the delivery man walked past with a happy tune on his lips, Asher pounced out from hiding, gave him a sharp blow on the back of his neck and dragged him into their hiding spot.

"He's out cold alright, but he'll be fine in time. Quick, get into the trolley."

Soon, there was a delivery man in white overalls with a trolley full of boxes once again approaching the big, grey building.

Beneath the boxes, Maryna whispered, "You're squashing my hand."

The Captain leant forward quickly. "I *do* beg your pardon."

"Shhh," said Asher as he approached the gate confidently. He pressed the numbers in one after the other, without hesitation, as though he'd done it a thousand times before. And soon after he'd finished, a whole section of the gate slowly slid along the ground to the left, leaving a wide open space, with nothing ahead but the pathway leading all the way up to that large, glass door. When he was halfway up the path, the gates slid shut behind him, and when he stood at the door, it was opened to him. He entered with a huge grin on his face and from here, he knew exactly where to head.

From beneath the box, the Captain heard him say suddenly, "Delivery for A1."

Then another different voice said "Just drop it here."

"I had instructions to take it directly to A1 himself."

"Oh . . . very well. He'll be back soon. Wait here please."

The room where Asher had come to was now empty. "This is it," said Asher to the trolley. "What are you going to say to him, Captain?"

The Captain rose up from out of the trolley, lifting up the boxes and putting them aside. "I don't know yet. I usually make it up as I go along."

"I can't believe I'm here again," said Marnya, stepping out of the trolley. "And in *this* place. A1's lair."

"Worried?" the Captain asked her.

"Very. I'm worried about what A1's going to do to us when he sees us."

The Captain was looking around the room and couldn't see anything that gave away any clues as to how the place was run or how it might possibly be stopped. It was just a bare, circular room—like a foyer or grand hallway, with a shiny marble floor. It was like a waiting room and they were clients waiting to go in and fire the consultant.

After five minutes or so, a man came into the room and said that A1 had returned and a grand door was opened to them.

The Captain hadn't expected to be led straight to him—what a convenience. He would go in there and demand his friends to be released. Then he would demand an explanation as to this seemingly unethical establishment.

The grand door had led into a short, grand passageway and there was another door at the end of it, which opened before them without one of them having to touch a door knob. In the large room beyond, there was an oversized desk with a big high-back cushiony chair behind it in the centre of the room. The chair was facing away from the door and all that could be seen of the person sitting in it was the top of a balding head. All five visitors were inside the room. The chair slowly turned around and the enigmatic A1 was revealed in a dramatic, but suave way. He was quite ordinary looking. Nothing about his appearance was particularly frightening or sinister, but Marnya shivered and was filled with dread at the sight of him again. Asher, Jon and Pintz waited hungrily for what he was going to say.

A grin came across his face slowly and he eyed each person standing before him in turn. And when he did open his mouth to speak, it was certainly not what the Captain wanted to hear.

"Thank you, gentlemen," he said coolly. He was looking directly at Asher, Jon and Pintz. "You have done splendidly. It couldn't have been easy luring this strong-minded trouble-maker into my trap. He'll make a lovely addition to my collection."

He laughed with excitement. And then Asher, Jon and Pintz, all started walking forward to join A1 behind his desk.

"I'm not interested in the girl, you can send her to the Infirmary and she can be patched and taken back home. As I always say, there's no place like home."

While A1 was saying this, Pintz went over to a small box sitting on one section of the desk and spoke into it. "Can I have someone in here to take away a patient please?"

Both the Captain and Marnya were stunned. Marnya looked terrified, but the Captain looked more expressionless. All his infuriated feelings didn't feel like appearing on his face because he felt he shouldn't be feeling those feelings because he should have felt that something like this was happening all along.

Within seconds, there was a man and a woman dressed in black who came in to the room and grabbed Marnya—one on each arm—and whisked her out. She screamed and kicked and shouted and made an attempt to clasp onto the Captain in protest, but it was no use. Her screams and protests grew quieter and quieter as she was quickly marched away.

"What is this?" the Captain asked, disgusted at what was going on, while A1 merely sat there, contented.

"Z23, would you kindly explain?"

It was Asher who spoke, with no hint of remorse whatsoever. "A1 first tracked you wandering about on planet Zero early yesterday. He contacted me from the Sanctuary to . . ."

"To lie to me. All three of you are A1's agents. You work for him. I must say you're good at your job. Usually I can detect liars quite easily."

"I thought you might appreciate their skill."

"Appreciate it? Appreciate it?" The Captain had been able to control his anger up until now. "It's an utterly and totally . . . appallingly . . . *unpleasant* thing to do. What kind of parents did you have? Didn't they teach you anything? That liars don't go unpunished? And it hurts. To be lied to."

"Oh I'm sorry," A1 patronised. "Sorry that you appear to have lived such a sheltered life that you've never had the experience of being lied to. You clearly need to get out more."

"I never said I've never been lied to," the Captain said evenly, "I've had my share. And I've never seemed to manage to get through to the liar that it benefits them not one little bit in the end."

"It's a shame you couldn't get anymore of those poor lost souls out there to come with you," A1 said to Z23.

"I tried my best."

"Well we got three back. That's not bad to be going along with. And two new ones now as well!"

"What do you mean 'planet Zero'?" the Captain said. "Is *that* what this planet's called?"

"I've called it that," said A1. "Rather fitting don't you think. When one comes to the Sanctuary, they have zero worries, zero responsibilities, zero stress . . ." he was smiling cheerfully.

"Yes and zero *life* by the looks of things. Why do you do it? Why are you running this place? And why have you gone to so much trouble to bring me here?"

"Ah, well *you* were an interesting case. At first, you were just another potential addition to my collection. But after Z23 and the others, 1F90 and 206 had started interacting with you, I decided to test you out. Work out what kind of personality I was up against. The original plan was merely to lead you close enough to the zone of dimensional proximity for it to *snap you up*, but I thought I would have a little fun with you first. Now I know more about you and now I can create a more appropriate stay for you here in the Sanctuary."

"And what do you mean by collection? What *collection*?"

He looked amused, as if the answer was obvious. "*My* collection." He leant forward. "Of people."

Chapter Eleven

Time For A Check-Up

Evie was back home. Not her real home. Her *Sanctuary* home. She was eating some bread and jam at the kitchen table, staring out the window. There had been a content, but vacant smile on her face as she was eating her three o'clock snack. The outing she'd had with A1 had made her peckish. But now, as she began to chew slower and slower, her face was drooping slowly into a vague frown. Eventually, she stopped chewing altogether, looked up at the clock and couldn't believe her eyes. How could it have been three o'clock? It only felt like five minutes ago she was with Laura in the village square. Something on the fridge caught her eye. It was a note on a business card-sized leaflet. It wasn't there before.

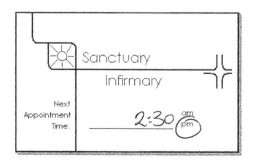

She pulled it off the fridge, looked at the clock again and realised the appointment time had passed. She couldn't even remember getting this little card from the Infirmary. But then, a picture flashed into her memory. A picture of that Recovery Room . . . and *Paulo*. Paulo had been there! She all of a sudden remembered that feeling. Of seeing him, but not being able to do anything about it—not quite understanding who he was. But *now* she knew who he was. Why couldn't she tell him back then? That, so far, was all she remembered. But she was beginning to understand a lot more now. She had obviously been 'patched' as Laura had put it. She'd conformed to their ways for a short time and now she needed a top up because it was wearing off.

"Well not today," she said out loud in the silent tomb of her house. She screwed up the little card and threw it in the peddle-bin.

But then all of a sudden, her house wasn't so silent. There was a band playing some music somewhere nearby. She had nothing else to do but sit around waiting to be rescued, so she went outside and down the end of the road to see what it was. Every few metres, the sound grew louder as she was getting closer to the music, and now that she could make out the tune, it made her feel uncomfortable. It was a brass band, but it was playing the most obscure and irritating melody. It was upbeat and happy sounding, yet somehow shady and twisted, as though someone was making a mockery of happiness.

She reached the end of the next road and finally saw what it was all for. There was a short procession of people, (about half of them musicians), all wearing black, walking down the road adjacent to where Evie was standing. In the centre of the procession, four people each held up a corner each of a simple wooden coffin. She got a shock. *I suppose people do still die here. An elderly lady or man probably—died of old age.*

She *was* going to just stand where she was and watch the procession go past slowly, but then she saw a stray walker, hardly able to go on from crying. No one was paying any attention to her so Evie decided to join her.

"Close friend of yours?" Evie asked gently.

The woman nodded, blubbing into a handkerchief. "She was someone I'd grown quite fond of. She was kind to me and she was probably the only one who didn't give me a rotten fake smile everyday. Poor Seven-B-Twelve."

7B12. 7B12. 7B12 . . .

The name went whirring around in Evie's head like a dizzying sandstorm. She forgot all about the woman standing in front of her and left without saying another word. All Evie wanted to do was storm into the Infirmary and ask what had happened to Laura!

When Evie arrived, there was a huge rigmarole at the front 'check-in' station—trying to get them to understand who it was she was talking about. She explained until she was blue in the face that there was just a funeral progression for her and finally they seemed to understand.

"You mean the *previous* 7B12?"

"She's been replaced?"

"Naturally. No I'm afraid the previous 7B12 was sadly taken by erm . . . let me see . . ." the nurse at the desk was looking up records on a clip board of information. "A speeding car. It was a tragic incident."

Evie was devastated, she could hardly speak. "You mean . . . you mean she was . . . hit?"

"Died instantly apparently. There was nothing the doctors could do I'm afraid." She spoke gently but somehow it was completely sympathy-deficient.

"I don't believe it," she said, half in a daze.

"You're due for a check-up aren't you?" the woman said all of a sudden, somehow knowing exactly who Evie was. "Let's see," she was looking up another clipboard full of records. "D14. Half past two." She looked up sharply at Evie with a slightly worried expression. There was a pause, and then . . . "You'd better come along with me."

Before the woman could even get a hold of her in any way, Evie was out of there like a shot. She knew what a 'check-up' would mean. She would be 'patched' again and sent into a dazed half-existence for the rest of the day. She couldn't let that happen again.

She didn't know *where* to run, but she knew she just had to! The most disturbing thing was that no one from the Infirmary ran after her. She thought of all those cameras in the streets, watching her, and realised they probably didn't need to chase her. They only had to watch. She could run for days and days, stop for a breath and find them waiting around the next corner.

She could look for Paulo! Where would he be? What was his number? C36—that's right. She would head for the 'C' houses, and surely she would come across him eventually . . . if he was home. She at least knew he was with her inside the Sanctuary somewhere.

After a few minutes however, she abandoned this idea. With this strategy, she never seemed to be getting away from the main streets and shops—the busiest areas, and therefore, the cameras. The words of Laura echoed in her head.

Head for the forest. Probably the safest place is the forest—no surveillance.

Well, she didn't have a clue what she was going to do once she got there, but she felt that it might be the best place at the moment. At least then she could get her breath back and think of a plan.

A good, solid, non-stop sprint later, she reached the edge of the main part of the village, where the trees began to get thicker. She was away from people, but not out of contact with the community. The next thing she heard was a voice on a loud speaker mounted on a street lamp. It was a male voice, but it didn't quite sound like the voice she knew belonged to A1.

It said:

Attention, citizens of the Sanctuary. First of all, I hope you're all enjoying this lovely day. But be on the look out for a runaway patient who is in urgent need of care from the Infirmary. She is a young girl of about thirteen or fourteen, has long dark hair, almost black, is wearing three-quarter jeans, a pink T-shirt, a white hooded jacket and fairly distinctive black and white striped socks. Her name is D14 and it is vital the Infirmary has her back in its care. If you spot her, please inform the authorities at once. Please do not try to approach her as she has shown unpredictable behaviour and may be dangerous. I repeat, citizens of the Sanctuary, it is absolutely vital this girl is found.

Evie realised she'd gotten away from the busy part of the Sanctuary just in time, and she knew that heading for the forest and hiding away was indeed the best plan.

Paulo wasn't quite sure why, but he was sitting in a room full of chairs with a table full of magazines in the middle of it. There were seven or eight others in the room sitting on chairs as well. Nobody communicating—just either sitting staring at the wall, or sitting staring at a magazine. It was a waiting room of some kind.

A nurse came in. "B618?"

A man stood up nervously and left the room with her. He was gone a while, and when he came out, Paulo could see him walk past the door when the nurse came in to get the next person. He had a big smile on his face and walked with a spring in his step.

"67A?"

This time, a woman stood up and followed the nurse out. She seemed less hesitant to do so—but not excited. Just as though it was a mundane task of having a dental check-up.

A few minutes later, the people in the waiting bay could hear a giggle. It was the woman on her way out. She looked as though a huge weight had been taken off her shoulders and she sighed and left.

"27KZ3?"

A big, stocky man stood up. This guy *was* hesitant. He had big furrows in his forehead and looked around cautiously before going with the nurse.

When he came out, he was thanking the nurse cheerfully and he didn't have a care in the world.

Paulo frowned.

"H41?"

An older man stood up and went with the nurse. When they were gone, Paulo decided to get up and stand by the door to try and get a closer look at the people on their way out.

Shortly, there was movement, and the old man went past, out through a hallway as the nurse came into the waiting bay again.

"C36?"

Paulo's eyes widened when he realised that on the man's upper arm was a small rectangle shaped sticker—bluey-green in colour.

"C36?"

That's the patch Asher and the bunch were talking about! Paulo thought. *I'm not having that!*

"C36!" the nurse repeated.

Paulo looked, wide-eyed. "Not me," he said when he noticed she was looking right at him.

The nurse frowned. "But I'm sure . . . Let me just go and check." She exited. She looked very young, probably new to the job. Paulo was grateful.

"I'm getting out of here," he announced to the people left in the room. "This is not natural. Does anyone want to join me? There's not much time. Pretty soon, that nurse'll come back realising C36 *is* me."

They stared up at him blankly with that look on their faces. The look you might unintentionally display when there's someone weird in the room. When you're uncomfortable because of their presence, but trying not to show it.

Paulo was confused and suddenly doubtful. It seemed like a good thing they were doing, but somehow, deep in the back of his mind, he couldn't help thinking it was the wrong way to go about it. He second guessed himself though—standing there on the spot, in indecision. *Maybe this* is *nothing but good. I mean, they're making people better aren't they? They're only doing kind. Should I stay and see what it's all about?*

115

He had only seconds to think, and he couldn't get rid of this uncomfortable feeling in the back of his head—and it *wasn't* where the mosquito had bitten him a few days ago back in ancient Jerusalem. It was that feeling—that something just wasn't right.

He ran for it, managing to leave that particular section of the Infirmary without being seen by the nurse. He stopped abruptly at the end of a corridor, not knowing which way to turn, and he suddenly thought it wise to stop running—it would only look more suspicious.

Left . . . or right?

He heard some voices coming from the left.

I guess it'll be right! he thought, and paced down that corridor. Unfortunately the voices weren't getting any quieter. Whoever they were, were following right behind him. He could hear them talking:

"I think I'll stay with him for a while and see what I can get out of him. What do you think Mark?"

"Yes, that's a very good idea Mark. Where are the records from the last patient?"

"Right here."

"Thank you, I'll take those to A1."

It kept on going for a while and Paulo felt sure they would catch up to him. Even if they didn't quite, they would at least come around the last corner and spot him in front of them. He had to think quickly. There were doors at various intervals down the corridor, and when he felt he had not one more second before they'd see him, he opened a door to his left and quickly ducked through it.

It opened onto yet another corridor, but it was more dimly lit than the last. And instead of the light being bright white, it was a dull shade of red, which gave him an uneasy feeling inside.

The doors lining this corridor had round porthole-like windows in them, and the temptation was too strong for Paulo—he looked through the glass of the first door he came to . . .

He regretted it immediately. The sight was most odd. The room beyond was also lit red, but it was a deeper, darker red and there were eight or so people in there, sitting on the floor around the edges of the room—their backs against the wall and their legs stretched out in front of them. The *really* weird part though, was that they were laughing—as though trying out different kinds of laughs. Paulo didn't know whether to smile or frown. It made him feel so uneasy that he quickly moved further down the corridor and up to the next door. And the view through this one was just as strange. It was lit in blue this time and there were people walking slowly in a line behind a smartly dressed woman in a skirt suit. (Paulo tried to stay well out of her sight). They were following after her taking one slow step after another—calmly and carefully—as if they were playing a child's game of "Follow the Leader". Paulo couldn't hear anything but it looked as though the woman in the front was speaking to them—giving instructions on how to walk.

He moved further down the corridor, shaking his head in disbelief. Then there were more sounds from behind him. He froze—firstly, trying to work out whether there were actually people coming his way, and secondly, to work out which way to run.

He came to the end of the red corridor and there was just a big door–no continuation of the corridor. Going back the way he came would only expose him to whoever was coming fast behind him. He was boxed in. He had to enter one of the rooms. But which door? He considered straight away that the one he entered might also be the one the people behind him wanted to enter. But he had to take a chance. The one straight ahead at the end of the corridor was the door he silently opened, passed through and silently closed again behind him.

This room was black. Actually pitch black—he couldn't see a thing. He listened by the door for the voices, and they seemed to get louder but luckily, quieter again until they eventually faded altogether with the sound of a different door closing somewhere nearby. He breathed a silent sigh of relief. Then he wondered about his surroundings. Just what kind of room what *this* going to be? It was silent as well as dark, which settled him a bit. He found a light switch with his fingers, flicked it on . . . and was amazed.

The platform on which he was standing looked out onto a massive, wide open room. There were about five steps directly in front of him that led down into the place and without thinking, he walked down them—one, two, three, four, five. The room was sectioned off into hundreds of little compartments, separated by dark curtains, and in each of them was a screen, a couple of filing cabinets and a small table—sometimes with documents and books and things laid out on them.

As he passed each compartment, there was always something happening on every screen but the sound was muted. They were movies of mundane events played out by ordinary people, almost like hundreds of reality T.V. shows and each from just one person's point of view—as if the camera was inside the person's eyes. And one thing he noticed was that often, the people visible on the screen looked worried or confused every time they looked into the 'camera'.

He must have walked passed at least fifty of them—on either side of him. As he walked along he noticed each compartment was labelled with a letter-number combination, and soon, he came across a compartment labelled C36. He frowned and swallowed as he approached the compartment, sectioned off with a thick black curtain. On the screen . . . was his old workplace on Serothia. He knew it was the exact place and not a copy (like his home in the Sanctuary) because occasionally one of his workmates would walk past and give 'the camera' a queer look. Sometimes, on would come a view of a piece of Satellite equipment being worked on—full screen.

Paulo looked away and sat on a chair by the table, confused about what he was seeing. He leant his elbow on the table and bumped something. Suddenly, someone called his name.

"Paulo? Paulo?"

He looked up. Nobody was around. But then, when he looked at the screen again, he realised who it was and where they were. It was one of his work friends, Squirt. [*]

"Paulo, are you sure you're feeling alright? You don't look good. I mean, I don't mean that in a nasty way, I mean, normally you look great. I'm sure you're quite a handsome lad, although I wouldn't know, you know, being another lad and everything, but I'm sure young ladies

---

[*] 'Squirt' was a nickname for him. His actual name was Haron and he got to know Paulo quite well when together they helped save Serothia from a swarm of blue blob creatures who wanted to take over their planet. I'll warn you now, Squirt had a habit of talking quite a lot—using a hundred words in a sentence, when two would do.

would think so. But today, you just don't look . . . very well. And yesterday as well, come to think of it."

Then, Paulo got the ultimate surprise when he heard his own voice come out in reply to his friend Squirt on the screen. "I'm alright, really. Leave me alone."

The voice was quite monotone in pitch and almost mechanic in rhythm. Paulo frowned, knowing he'd never talk to Squirt like that.

Squirt looked taken aback and hurt. He backed away carefully and said, "Sorry. Just concerned that's all."

"Just let me get back to work." And the view went back to the piece of equipment being worked on.

Paulo was frozen to the spot, just staring up at the screen in disbelief. *Who is this imposter? It's certainly not me!*

He lunged forward and opened the filing cabinet next to the screen and a file he picked up from the front said 'PAULO VISTAR' along the top with the code 'C36' next to his name and then a whole heap of information underneath.

"Paulo, will you come to my office please?" came another voice suddenly, and on the screen, *Paulo substitute* walked down some corridors and entered the boss' office. ♣

I won't bore you with everything Paulo's boss said to the Paulo substitute, but it wasn't good news. He concluded by saying:

"You're no longer getting along with your colleagues, you're slapdash in your work, you haven't arrived on time

---

♣ It was a man the real Paulo had not yet met because the previous boss was tragically murdered by one of the Satellite trainees who was under the influence of those blue blob creatures.

since you came back from that Satellite SB-17 mission. I don't think I can rely on you much longer."

Paulo substitute said in a very plain, emotionless voice, "Give me another chance. I will do everything you ask of me."

"I'm not sure I can take the risk. But alright one more chance. But you're on your last leg, Vistor. One more complaint from employees and you're *out!*"

Paulo's mouth dropped. "That's my job you're ruining!" he yelled at the screen. "Let me get back there! That's my life!!"

He couldn't watch anymore. He found the button he bumped before and the sound went off again. He decided to pop his head into some of the other compartments and he heard many other disturbing sounds and fragments of conversations:

"You don't even *care* anymore. What's happened to you? You're like an empty shell."

"Are you listening? Fine, if you're going to act like that, then we're through!"

"Sometimes I feel like you're just not the same person anymore. I think we should go our separate ways."

"You're fired. You've got no passion for this company anymore."

"I don't know why you're acting this way, but I think you should leave and never come back."

"The children and I need you to be part of this family!"

"Here, have this and put yourself out of your own misery!"

"Is anybody in there? Speak to me!"

"You're not the man I fell in love with."

"You can live on the streets, see if I care!"

. . . And it went on and on and on. These were clearly people's lives. The people who were living in the Sanctuary. Their *real* lives. And they were all heading for catastrophe, misery and tragedy.

Chapter Twelve

The Collector And The Protector

Normal people have rock collections, shell collections, key ring collections and stamp collections. (The Captain had even known somebody with a letter box collection.) But a people collection? That *had* to be the most bizarre one he'd come across. Not to mention the most unethical.

By now, Asher, Jon and Pintz (or rather Z23, 1F90 and 206) had left A1 alone with the Captain.

"So, let me get this straight," said the Captain, pacing around the over-sized desk of the big round sumptuous office. "This whole place is basically a storage place for your collection?"

"Oh, I'm not sure I like the way you put it. It's much more than that."

The Captain took a new breath. "Alright then. I'm game. *What* is it exactly?"

"It's a *paradise*," he almost whispered. "Where people can escape from life. You know how it is. How *busy* life can become. People are so *stressed*, they've no time to rest, relax, enjoy life's pleasures. And I'm sure you know how beneficial rest is. How productive one can be when one is rested."

"Yes but, productive for what. They don't do anything here. And they never will by the looks of it. Once people are here, they don't come out. That's the gist I seem to have picked up so far."

"People never want to go back to reality after a holiday. You ask anyone. Back to routine, back to work, back to school. It depresses them. Why have that depression when you don't have to? I'm doing these people a favour. I'm saving them. I'm offering them a sanctuary."

"You're not *offering* it, your forcing it on them whether they want it or not."

"Everybody wants it. Some may not realise, but deep down inside, everybody has the desire for *rest*."

"There's a time for everything, A1. A season for every activity under heaven. Of course people want rest. But you can't do that twenty-four hours of the day and seven days of the week."

"But of course, they do things other then rest. They have jobs in the village as shop keepers, taxi drivers, waiters and cooks. But it's all restful. They all enjoy doing it. I don't force them to work if they don't wish. Everybody you see doing something, they're doing it because they want to. They see it as a service back to me for what I have provided for them."

"Are you sure about that?"

"Of course."

The Captain tried a different tact. "You know life's not *all* stress. There are good moments. Restful moments. Happy, peaceful, relaxing moments without the use of your . . . facility. I will admit that some people stack their lives up too much with work, but the aim is to have a good balance. I don't think you have a good balance here."

"You're missing a vital point, Captain, and here I must return to our initial discussion. It's not just about the people in my collection. It's about my collection. They're here for *me*. I merely try and make it comfortable here for them. I provide easy living. But what *I* get out of it, is much greater and much more important."

"And what's that?"

"I've already told you. It's my collection. My collection is my life. I may as well tell you; this place started out as a temporary resort for people to come for a holiday. Over the years I enjoyed hearing stories of why people chose to come here, what brought them to the decision to take a break, and they *interested* me—all those lives and motives for doing what they do. Over time, I realised how everybody could do with a holiday, but one of a more permanent nature. I always hated seeing people go when it was time for their holiday to end. I saw their depression of the thought of going back to routine . . . and I felt *my* depression . . . when they left . . .

"Anyway, I've developed a real hobby for collecting people now. The thrill of catching them. The challenge of finding new and better ways of luring them in. And then seeing the joy and happiness on their faces when they realise they have nothing to ever worry about ever again. It's priceless. And I wouldn't give that up for anything."

He got up and walked over to one of the walls of his office, pressed a button, and a whole section of the wall slid back effortlessly, revealing a huge screen behind it. On the screen was live surveillance showing a hallway of the Infirmary—and the Captain recognised Paulo straight away, walking cautiously down it. [*]

"This young chap for example, resisting what I'm offering him here. He's *just so interesting*, don't you think. I'm glad I've got him. He makes for quite good entertainment. Look at him, wandering about in a staff-only zone."

The Captain pretended not to recognise him. "Aren't you going to catch him?"

"I want to see what he does first." A1 was watching as if it was his evening television viewing. The only thing missing was the popcorn.

Paulo just heard the pair of nurses approaching through the corridor and coming straight for him, so he looked for a way to turn.

There was an alert signal coming from a sort of control deck underneath the big screen.

"Ah!" said A1 cheerfully. "A new case by the sound of it!" He pressed a different button, and the screen changed from Paulo looking for an escape, to what looked like another office—a consulting room with a lady consultant behind the desk, and a young woman sitting opposite her. The poor, depressed woman was saying:

"I feel so low at the moment, I just don't know what to do. I have so many things I *need* to do but I don't know where to start. I don't want to start at all, that's the problem. I just feel like going to bed, curling up with my head under the blanket and staying there for a whole month."

---

[*] In case you were wondering, this is before he entered that strange corridor with the red lighting.

A1 was nodding and smiling. "Yes, yes, and so you shall, don't you worry. Sounds like she needs a sanctuary, wouldn't you agree, Captain?"

He wasn't given the opportunity to answer.

A1 held a button down and spoke into a little microphone. "Sue, A1 here. Take your client into your portal room, (remember, *client* not patient). Bring her to the Sanctuary. She'll *love it!*" He smiled, rubbed his hands together and skipped back over to his desk. "She'll be a lovely new addition. She looks like she could be a little bit of a trouble-maker, but we'll get her straightened out."

He laughed greedily, and started making some notes on a piece of paper at his desk.

The Captain couldn't get the frown off his face. He looked back at the big screen and watched, as the poor woman was led into a little side room off the consulting room. Then came a flash of light that could be seen through the small crack under the closed door, and that screech that he'd heard when Evie was taken.

The sun was getting lower in the sky, but Evie was too afraid to come out of the forest yet and go home. There didn't seem to be any danger here, not like what you'd expect in a forest. It was quite dark underneath the thick canopy of trees but at the same time, there were little pools of light dolloped here and there along the straight passageways of the forest created by standing street lamps up against some of the trees. When Evie took the time to notice, the place was really quite beautiful. There were pleasant sounds all around—of birds hurrying home before night fell, crickets beginning their distant calls, the gentle breeze pushing through the leaves. One could really relax here. There were no sounds of frightening creatures like one normally hears in the woods. Not even any creepy crawlies on the ground. It was as if the whole place was being maintained in some kind of artificial way. Evie was aware of how pleasant it all must have been, but this is not the way she felt, deep down inside. She couldn't settle and appreciate the pleasantness, because the only thing she seemed to be able to focus on was how she was going to get away. The calmness therefore, only made her more agitated. The peaceful stillness was a new kind of torture. She felt trapped—just as much as she did before, possibly even more so. And she felt helpless and alone . . . and cold.

She sneezed suddenly and hoped she wasn't catching a cold. Her ears were ringing. The silence started to become like noise in her head, her calm and almost fantasy-like surroundings were beginning to make her feel sick and she found it was better to keep moving to allow the air to flow over her cheeks. She wandered and wandered and wandered around—not knowing where she wanted to get to—not even sure that she wasn't going around in circles. It was getting darker, she knew that much. And, come to think of it, the lamps seemed to have become a lot less frequent. They were now behind her, and thicker forest darkness was ahead of her.

She knew she'd wandered deeper into the forest when soon she came across a dark pool of water in the ground—about a metre in diameter. She was terribly thirsty, but she hesitated because as she approached closer, the water actually looked black and as she lent over it, there was no reflection staring back at her.

Maybe it just looks dark because it's night time, she thought. She knelt down beside it and dipped the very tip of her finger in. She pulled it out again and dabbed her finger on the tip of her tongue. She was perplexed . . . her fingertip wasn't wet. She dipped her finger in again, this time, plunging it in a little further. She swirled it around a bit, then pulled it out again and examined it. It was dry. And it took her a little while to notice also, that her finger had made no ripples in the water.

I should stop calling it water at this point, because indeed as you've probably guessed, it was not water at all. And it was about now that Evie realised it was not water. When she placed her whole hand in, it felt like . . . nothing. Just as though she was poking her hand through the air.

Suddenly, she had to sneeze again, unexpectedly—you know the way it sometimes creeps up on you and then takes you by surprise as if jumping out and saying BOO!

It was so much of a surprise that she lost her balance, and fell right into the pool . . . no splash and no noise.

Instead of being completely submerged in water, trying to hold her breath and tread her way up to the top again, she was doing a summersault on dry ground. When her body stopped rolling and she got back up onto her feet, she looked around, completely puzzled. She was still in the forest . . . or more accurately, still in *a* forest. But it had changed. It was much darker than before, and the sounds weren't so pleasant. She heard an owl screeching in the distance somewhere—its short spooky night call that sounds like a distressed scream. Then she heard flapping of wings and she imagined bats up in the trees. She looked back to try and see where she had come from, but she couldn't recognise any of it. She did see a funny kind of tree up ahead though—a very distinctive one. It had a huge hollow part in the middle of its trunk. And in the hole was a strange, subtle oddity. She thought it must have been a trick of the moonlight, but as she approached, it was quite clear before her eyes. The oddity was, that inside the hole was black, instead of showing a view of the other side of the tree. She reached out to put her hand through the hole, and to her surprise, her hand disappeared—as if she had dipped it into a pool of water again.

"It must be some kind of . . . portal," she said to herself, in disbelief. With hesitation again, she leant forward and put her head face-down through the hole this time . . .

And *then* she saw the forest she was in before, but the amazing thing was, where she expected to see the forest floor, was actually a regular view of the forest you would get if you were standing upright and looking straight ahead. The old forest that she was standing in before was tipped ninety degrees. (Or was it this one that was tipped ninety degrees?) Anybody standing in the old forest would have seen a head protruding upwards out of the black pool Evie had been kneeling by earlier.

She quickly pulled her head back out through the hole of the tree trunk and could not fathom what was going on. She kind of knew. She thought that she must have just passed through a window from one dimension to another. Perhaps she had just exited the Sanctuary! Evie hoped it was not just wishful thinking. She knew that the old forest and the new forest were definitely in different

dimensions because of the weird 'Escher Painting' effect.♣
And the two forests were certainly very different.

Speaking of which, she suddenly got a cold shiver
running down her spine when she thought she heard
footsteps, and then the panting of a very large, probably
very dangerous animal. Big paddy paws plodding along
the leafy forest floor and her eyes darted this way and
that to try and work out which direction it was in. She
heard the rustling of some foliage to her left and so ran
suddenly to her right. She immediately regretted running,
because she thought she heard the footsteps of the animal
speeding up now to pursue her.

Evie's footsteps were echoed by the animal's
footsteps—and she could hear them galloping now. What
was it? A lion? A tiger? A bear?

"Oh my!" she shrieked, and ran faster than she ever
thought she could. She came across a giant tree with a
small hole towards the bottom of it. She knocked on the
tree and heard that it was hollow and with a quick glance
behind her to see whether the animal had caught up
with her yet, she ducked down into the hole and found a
small hiding place for herself. When she rested, panting,
against the back of the tree trunk, there was a violent
flutter of wings and she screamed in reflex, flailing her
arms about to get whatever it was away from her. A bat
flapped around her head until it found its way out and
flew away.

♣   Escher was a famous artist who painted strange dimensionally
obscure paintings. Scenes that were often also optical illusions
that could only ever exist on two-dimensional paper and not
in three-dimensional reality. Evie had learnt about him in
Art at school.

She breathed deeply in and out to try and catch her breath—silently. Then, in that cold, musty and lonely tree trunk, she started to cry. She covered her face with her dirty hands and sobbed for a while, starting to get a horrible gloomy feeling that she might never get home.

Evie thought suddenly of the Sanctuary, and felt so relieved that she was out of there—or pretty sure she was. She no longer had that stale, trapped feeling she'd always had in the Sanctuary. The air felt different—not so clean and fresh, but just . . . normal. She exhaled a huge breath of air from her lungs and looking up into the gloom of the tree trunk. She hated to imagine what creepy crawlies might be in there with her, but she refused to think about it. She closed her eyes, letting the tear drops run freely down her cheeks and neck.

"God," she said softly, (so as not to attract her pursuer). "Please keep me safe. I know I don't talk to you very often, so I don't even know if I deserve good things. I know that you sent your Son to die for me so you must care about me . . . a lot. And I know that in some weird, wacky way, You and Jesus are the same person. One day I'll have to try and get my head around that. But all I want to understand now is that You're with me and You're protecting me."

She thought about Jesus then, for a long while. How He came into the world as a baby and lived as a human being, so that He could sympathise with human difficulties, human struggles, human fears, temptations and insecurities. So that He could understand how she felt right now. She supposed that Jesus felt alone many times and she was comforted by that thought. She was talking to someone who'd been there, done that.

The funny thing then was, Evie felt calm and peaceful for the first time in a *long* time. Here, in this terrifying forest, with bats lurking in the shadows and who-knows-what hunting her down outside, she felt relaxed—more than she'd ever felt in the comfort of her own home in the so-called 'Sanctuary'. Here, in this empty carcass of a tree, where she knew Jesus was listening and sympathising with her, was a much realer sanctuary.

Chapter Thirteen

What's On Telly?

Another new arrival in the Sanctuary. A young woman not knowing where to turn in her life

"She'll fit right in," A1 was saying. "There she is, see? Being carried to one of the recovery beds. She'll feel all refreshed in a moment."

"She'll feel all confused," the Captain corrected him.

"You're quite a negative person aren't you?"

"Only when I see something to be negative about. What's going to happen to that woman after she wakes up?"

"She'll be taken to the Recovery Room for a little while to get her bearings, then sent to her new home. I'll have a chat with her in the next few days to welcome her and explain everything. Then . . . well, she's set up for a care-free relaxing life here. It's clever isn't it?"

"So that's it then. She's here for the rest of her life. It's a prison."

"It's helping people."

"What about Evie? What about Paulo and probably hundreds of others who just stumbled in? They didn't ask for it. They didn't need your *help*. Why don't you let them go?"

A1 raised his thumb and forefinger up to his forehead. "Oh dear, dear, I *have* explained this to you already. You see my theory is that *everyone* needs help, even if they don't admit it. And by the way, I don't know names, only codes. It's much easier that way. For instance, a bunch of people before they come here could have the same name—a nightmare! I have a code for *you* too, of course. You're going to love it. From now on you are A7."

"Why such a low number. I thought it'd be something higher, since you have so many in your *collection*."

"Well, since you seem a little more intelligent than most of my specimens, I thought the least I could do was give you a more superior code. The code A7 used to belong to one of the early settlers, but he's passed on since—natural causes of course—and that means we can re-use the code."

"I'm not sure I like the idea of having a second hand code."

"Too bad, dear chap. Come this way please." He started moving out of the room.

"What if I refuse to come with you?"

"You either cooperate . . . or you get the patch. I'm sure Z23 told you all about that."

He shuddered. "Yes I've . . . been well briefed about that."

"Then come this way," he said with a friendly smile—always friendly. "We have to show you to your new home."

Paulo couldn't get out of that particular room of monitored lives quick enough. One: because of the dreaded thought that any second, someone could walk in and discover him there; and two: he could no longer stand hearing his own voice saying careless comments he would never normally say, or *not* hearing his voice say something that he *would* say.

He managed to get back out to the main, brightly lit hallway where he came from without anybody seeing him. However, when he was out in the open again, there was another bunch of people coming his way—he could hear their voices. He quickly ducked behind the corner of an adjacent hallway and watched them approach. It was a small group of three men, dressed in white doctors' coats, entering another staff only section.

Paulo rested his head back against the wall with a sigh of relief that they hadn't seen him. In doing this, he saw out of the corner of his eye, some other white coats hanging on hooks along the wall next to him.

I need to find out more, he said to himself, took in a deep breath, and then before he could change his mind, he lifted a coat from its hook and quickly put it on. He slid his arms in the sleeves, untucked the collar, tried to put on a bold, official expression, and scurried across the hallway to open the staff-only door and join the others.

The three men walking down this next corridor became four men—walking into an elevator. The others didn't seem to notice. They all carried on in their usual manner rather professionally as if they were expecting a forth. When the lift stopped, Paulo got a rush of butterflies, thinking about what might have been in front of him when the doors opened. And he almost fainted when the doors did open and he realised he'd been brought straight into A1's office. He'd seen pictures and portraits of A1 here and there throughout the Sanctuary. He knew straight away that this had been a bad idea.

However, all A1 said was: "Ah, there you are. Will you please show A7 the way out, get him some transport and send him to his new home. The details are here." He handed one of them a piece of paper.

Then Paulo got a start when A7 was brought forward. It was *the Captain!* Paulo tried so hard not to have some display of recognition on his face, as did the Captain. They both kept their heads down.

"Thank you so much," A1 went on. "And be careful with him. He's a special case. Perhaps one of you could ride along with him. Make sure he gets there okay."

The four men indicated their understanding by dipping their heads, (one a second or two after the others) and the Captain was escorted out through the doors of A1's office building, down the lush plant-lined pathway and to the closest main road.

"Why four of you?" the Captain stirred. "I'm not some raging animal."

"A1 said you're to be very well looked after. It's for security."

"Oh, how nice."

They got him a vehicle and Paulo was quick to take charge. "I'll go with him," he said to the other three men.

He didn't expect it to be so easy. They said 'alright', gave him the piece of paper and that was it. Soon enough, the Captain and Paulo were seated together in the back seat of the vehicle, and being driven away.

The trip was silent. They both knew better than to speak yet. The driver had been given the directions and they just waited patiently until they arrived at their destination.

Their destination was a small pokey little house. Modern and well maintained, but with fine pieces of antique-looking furniture, not unlike the carriage room of the Train. However quaint it was, Paulo and the Captain didn't hang around to observe and admire the place. As soon as the driver left, they darted inside and checked the place over—making sure they were not going to be overheard or spied on. Without taking any chances though, the Captain found a wireless radio (one that was very familiar to him from his childhood) and turned it on loudly. He also started behaving as though he was being shown his new home by Paulo, and Paulo quickly caught on and acted like a doctor helping the Captain settle in.

"How did you get in?" was the first thing Paulo said to the Captain, under the sound of the radio.

"By Train."

"Oh. Well it was weird, the last thing I remembered was when I was talking to you out on that green grass and stopping you from being pulled in and then the next thing I was . . ."

"Waking up in a bed and then being taken to a Recovery Room?"

"Yes . . . Did that happen to you too?"

"I know what goes on. A1 showed me. By the way, we saw you earlier—roaming around the hallways of the Infirmary."

"No."

"Oh yes. But don't worry, we didn't see much. A1 was distracted by a new arrival."

"That's another strange thing. I was in the Infirmary, and when I came out from that lift, we were in a completely different . . ."

"You came out into A1's main office. The two buildings must be connected underground." While he was speaking the Captain was now pacing around the front room looking for . . . whatever he was looking for. (Paulo was content to just let him get on with it rather than ask questions.)

While he was doing that, Paulo saw a box in the corner that looked like a T.V.♣ "I wonder what's on telly," he said and flicked it on. The Captain appeared to show interest in Paulo's idea and he came over to watch over his shoulder.

The first thing that came on was a cooking show with some bored looking chef showing viewers how to boil water. Paulo changed the station and on came a soap opera.

"Oh R47 why did you have to do that? You know I love you already."

"But I've never really felt that you've accepted me for who I am. I always thought you wanted J22P."

"J22P could never make me happy. It's you I love. No matter what 37F9 says. I just want the old R47 back. I want you to be true to yourself."

"G90, that's the kindest thing anyone's ever . . ."

The Captain reached across and changed the station, and it was a murder mystery.

"H18, I'm arresting you on suspicion of the murder of 414. Do you have anything to say?"

"I'm innocent, Inspector 789! Please believe me!"

He changed the station again.

♣ Televisions looked slightly different on Serothia than on Earth.

"Cleaning your teeth can be so stressful can't it! That's why, believe it or not, you at home can have one of these top of the range automatic teeth-cleaning ensembles, which will do the magic for you while you're fast asleep. The first ten callers will receive fifty percent off and their reliability is guaranteed!"

He changed it over again.

"Hello. My name is Sue. And isn't it another beautiful day! Here in the Sanctuary we try and provide a stress-free environment. But sometimes our thoughts wander back to those days when you had so much on your mind. If this is you, I'm going to give you a few hints on how to stay calm and relaxed."

The Captain quickly changed it again.

"And in the latest news; a new arrival to the Sanctuary has found a happy ending in a new luxury two bedroom unit. She's known as D14 and if you see her in town, be sure to say a friendly 'hello'. Also making news . . ."

This made Paulo's ears prick up. "D14?" he said out loud and confused. "That's not her."

The Captain recognised the new comer as the woman he saw on the screen in A1's office. "What's the problem?" he asked.

"It's not Evie!"

"Well of course it's not Evie. Evie wouldn't be a newcomer."

"But she was D14!"

Suddenly, the Captain's face became serious and he was very interested. He moved closer to the television screen for more information, but by then, they'd moved on to different news. He frowned and straightened up, starting to feel very confused, but then there was a mix of both hope and dread.

"If there's now another D14," he said quietly, still staring at the screen, "then that means her code's being reused, and that means she's been replaced and *that* means . . ."

"What Captain?"

He looked straight at Paulo, wide-eyed. "She's no longer here. And she could be in terrible danger, in fact . . . we might already be too late."

Chapter Fourteen

What Happened To Evie?

It was the Captain who had bolted out of the house first, leaving Paulo asking urgent questions.

"What do you plan to do, Captain?"

"I plan to ask A1 what happened to Evelyn."

"What, just like that? I don't want him to see me. He might capture me again and put me back in that waiting room."

"What waiting room?"

"People were waiting to have patches put on their arm. I got well away from there."

"Good boy."

"Yeah but . . . what am I going to do when A1 sees me?"

"I don't know, but you should still come along with me. The more I get to know this place, the more I think that we should never split up."

They were doing all their talking while sprinting along—right into the main part of the Sanctuary. They were making a 'B-line' for A1's office building, but they were stopped in the street by a voice that pierced straight through them.

"Getting some exercise? What a good idea."

They turned around to see A1, sitting at a table outside a café, having a chilled glass of iced-tea. "I suppose it's like you said A7, there's a time for everything. Resting," he pointed to his glass, "and activity," he pointed to them.

"We're not out for a Sunday jog," said the Captain indignantly, walking over to him. "We're out to find you actually."

"Oh, how delightful. What can I do for you?" A1 raised his hand forward, directing the Captain to the seat opposite him.

The Captain did sit down and looked A1 straight in the eye. "What happened to Evelyn?"

"I'm sorry?"

"*D14* then. Where is she?"

"I assume you mean the *previous* D14." He lowered his head and shook it gently. "She was a friend of yours I take it. I'm afraid there's been a terrible tragedy. You see, late yesterday afternoon, she went for a swim. A deadly fish was spotted, you may have heard of a Great White Shark before . . . and . . . she was never seen again."

"What?" Paulo said, without being able to control himself.

"Oh you," said A1. "I thought I recognised you earlier. You're A7's other friend. Well, you two might as well settle down here now. Make it your home. Let us take care of you. I know how awful it is to lose a friend. Naturally we'll have a proper funeral service for her. You won't be disappointed."

"Oh yes and who conducts that?" said Paulo, suddenly getting angrier and angrier. "Sue? Mark? Or will it be Sue? Or perhaps Mark? Or any of the other brainless Marks and Sues you've got working here?"

"I don't believe you," the Captain said, taking no notice of Paulo's outburst. He hadn't taken his eyes off the smug, red-nosed man.

"I'm sorry?"

The Captain was as calm as a Sunday afternoon. "You want to know what *I* think happened? I think D14 found a way of getting out of here. I think she escaped. And because you'd never dream of broadcasting that on the news, you've made up some phony story as an explanation of why she's not here anymore"

A1 lowered his eyes, looking melancholy. "I'm sorry A7, but it's true. We all have our own way of dealing with the loss of a loved one and I understand that telling yourself that she's still alive might help for a little while . . ."

The Captain just got up off the chair and left his company, striding off—well out of his presence. Paulo followed right behind him.

"Well?" Paulo said after a short brisk walk. "Is it just wishful thinking or do you honestly disbelieve him?"

"*It's true*, he says," said the Captain. "What is truth coming from him? He hasn't given me one good reason since I met him to believe anything he says."

Paulo uneasily started telling the Captain something he ought to have known. "The last time I saw Evie . . . something had happened to her. They'd given her a patch probably and she was just like all these other mindless puppets walking around. In the state she was in . . . she'd never have tried to escape. What if she . . . did go for a swim . . ."

"Just stop there. I can't hear you."

It was when a sharp piece of sunlight came streaming in through the opening of the tree trunk, that Evie realised she had been asleep. Her mouth was dry and her feet were cold and she took a few moments to compose herself before she cautiously peeped her head out of the shelter she'd taken refuge in the previous night. There appeared to be nothing dangerous out there now. Whatever had been pursuing her last night had obviously either found some easier prey elsewhere or gotten too tired of looking and given up. She climbed out and brushed herself off. She wondered what her hair must look like. Luckily, by nature, Evie wasn't the type of person to worry about vanity above important things.

She looked at the dense forest all around her and wondered what she should do. When you're lost in a supermarket, they always tell you to stay put so that there's more chance of mum or dad coming around eventually and finding *you*. But if she stayed put *here*, she might be destined to spend the rest of her life staring at the trees by day and escaping the man-eating beasts by night.

Starting to feel hot and tingly all over from worry,[*] she said out loud, "God, what should I do?"

She was standing there for about half a minute and there was no reply. Why couldn't God just use one of those big, booming voices and say something clearly like how everyone imagines in happened in the Bible? Soon however, there did come a sound. Not a big, booming voice but a small, pretty voice. It was a bird. Evie had never heard a bird-song so beautiful before. She

---

* Like that rush of hot butterflies you used to get in the supermarket when for a quick few seconds you do lose your mum.

instinctively looked up to the trees to try and find which bird it was. The trees were too thick and she couldn't see anything, until her eyes rested on a low branch a little distance away to her left.

It was quite an ordinary looking bird really, so for a second she thought it couldn't have been the one. But when it opened and closed its beak, the beautiful sound came trickling out from it. She moved slowly toward it, to try and get a closer look—a smile finally making its way to her lips as every moment, it pitched a new note that sounded fit for a solo part in a Philharmonic Orchestra. One more step she dared to take, but it was a mistake. Her foot broke through some loose bracken on the forest floor and in a split second, it seemed that the ground gave way underneath her, she gasped, the bird flew away and she was falling.

It wasn't until she landed on a hard concrete floor, that she realised she'd actually tumbled down some steps and at the top of those steps was an old cellar door she'd come through—covered over by overgrown vines and mouldy leaves.

It was very dark down here. When she got up to look around, she could only see a few feet in front of her. The rest was in darkness.

Now, she could easily have walked back up those steps to an environment she was at least used to, but her curiosity got the better of her. She walked a little further into the darkness, the eerie silence haunting her bones. She didn't have far to roam until she came across a little pool of dull light hovering over the concrete floor. Someone was sitting there, legs crossed on an old mattress. Alone. Facing away from her. Evie's stomach lurched and her heart boomed loudly in her chest. She stepped silently closer and plucked up the courage somehow to say a little feeble, "Hello?"

The figure did not move, as if it . . . she hadn't heard her. It was definitely a girl. One step closer, and Evie suddenly recognised the side of her face.

"Laura!" she yelled out and ran straight to her. Still, it was as if Laura had not heard her voice, but as Evie got within a metre of her, Laura did then turn around and see her. Laura looked so weary and cold, and so surprised to see Evie.

She spoke but no sound came out. It was like a weird dream. Evie was no lip-reader, but she could tell Laura was trying to say her name, and after that, it looked like *help me.*

Then when Laura raised her hands up and they appeared to press up against an invisible wall, Evie realised she *was* saying stuff—probably calling out at the top of her voice, but Evie just couldn't hear her. There was an invisible and sound-proof barrier between them.

Evie noticed, that next to the mattress, there was also a chair, a small flask of water, and to her disgust, a toilet and a small basin next to it. The whole time Evie was staring at all this, Laura was still shouting at her hopelessly, trying to communicate something. Evie tried to work out what she was saying.

"What? What? I can't . . . What are you saying?"

She'd given up using her mouth to speak and was now making gestures. She was pointing at something above Evie and then she wiggled her finger in a way you might do to depict a worm. When Evie clearly wasn't understanding, she tried the words again.

Witch, it looked like, *witch? Why would she be saying witch?*

"Did a witch put you in here?" said Evie. Then she said to herself, "No, that's silly."

She watched as Laura then held up one hand vertically and then first used the index finger on the other hand to prod her palm, and then used her index finger and thumb to . . . draw on her palm? No . . . peel skin . . . no . . .

She watched her mouth carefully. Evie suddenly realised. *The switch! . . .*

What switch? Evie looked all over the place for one. Then she remembered where Laura had been pointing and she stood up and felt with her hands along the wall of the glass box. Right up the top in the shadows, which was far above head height for Evie, was the switch. She looked at Laura to indicate she'd found it. She wanted to check with her that she was meant to flick it and Laura seemed to be saying yes in a ridiculously exaggerated way.

When she flicked it, Laura came somersaulting out of the little glass box—she'd just been using the wall to lean against.

"Thank goodness you've come. How did you find me?"

"I don't know really. I kind of just . . . stumbled across you . . . literally."

"I was told no one would ever be able to find me."

"Well they lied obviously," Evie smiled. "What are you *doing* down here?"

"It's my new home sweet home."

"Doesn't look very sweet to me."

"You're kidding right? You think I *chose* to come down here?"

"I don't understand."

"I'll have to explain later."

"Well the opening's just over there, let's go!"

"We can't. Not yet."

"Why not?"

Laura, in reply, walked past Evie and over to another wall closer to the entrance. She seemed to know exactly where to go to find another collection of buttons and switches, even though they were all in darkness. She flicked one and said, "See for yourself."

On came hundreds of fluorescent lights everywhere. Rows and rows of them, flickering on one at a time so that a new section deeper into the underground room was revealed each second. Underneath the lights, Evie could now see, many people in the exact same predicament as Laura was in moments ago. Each in their individual tiny glass sound-proof box with their own little bed and their own little toilet.

Evie was speechless for a moment. All she could utter was, "Whoa." Then she managed to ask, "How did you know about those controls?"

"Because they come down here occasionally to feed us, to check on us, to add to us . . . to occasionally . . . take away a . . . body. I always paid attention to what they were doing."

"This is terrible! They're just left down here in the dark? Are all these people from the Sanctuary?"

Laura nodded. "When people persistently don't cooperate and there's no controlling them, they 'die' up there, and 'live' down here. A1 still owns us but we're out of the way so we don't cause any more trouble."

When the lights had come on, the hundreds of tired, pale, miserable people started looking around, first assuming it was another routine check or 'feeding time', but then, the ones closest to the entrance, were starting to realise that the people in charge were not the ones at the controls.

"And take a look at this!" said Laura, sidestepping to another array of controls, which was also next to a big screen mounted on the wall. She turned it on, typed in a random number-letter code on a keypad and then watched the screen.

There was an angry face in full view, looking straight at the camera, saying: "What's wrong with you? Don't you have any feelings at all?"

Laura typed in another code.

On the screen now was just a view of an empty, lonely room. A young man all dressed in white approached the 'camera' and handed forth a couple of pills and a little plastic cup of water.

Then Laura breathed in deeply and typed in 7B12—her own code. The screen changed to a view of a filthy looking street. The camera was close down to the pavers looking across the road onto some grotty looking buildings on the other side. From the view it showed, you could only see legs walking past and that's all that ever happened. Laura dipped her head slightly, then stared back up at the screen and said quietly and sadly, "I must be living on the streets back home. Or at least that's what it looks like." Then she swallowed and realised that she should explain to Evie. "They er . . . create a . . . an image of you. Or an android, or something false whatever it is, and they . . . replace you in the real world with that, while we live out our lives in the Sanctuary. I don't know why they bother, it wouldn't be any worse than to leave our friends and family wondering where we got to."

"But how do they know where we live and that?"

Laura shrugged. "I figured they might be scanning people's brains or something when they first enter the Sanctuary. That's how they can re-create exact copies of our homes here as well. Probably by reading our memories. He thinks it would make us feel more comfortable here, having a copy of our own home. But it's just the opposite don't you think."

Evie nodded glumly, staring unseeingly at the controls of the screen. She was thinking of her life back home—dying to see what was happening, but at the same time totally unsure of whether she *wanted* to see.

Laura, guessing what Evie was thinking, said gravely, "Go ahead."

Evie reached forward and slowly typed in D-1-4. There seemed to be a confusion of which one she meant. She had to choose between three different ones. But there was no doubt which one was hers when her mother came into full view on the screen. Evie could feel the warm swell of tears growing behind her eyes as she watched. She had to catch her breath when she felt her throat lock up.

Her mother didn't appear to be talking to Evie-substitute, but to someone else in another room. It looked like Evie-substitute was listening in to a private conversation.

"Her grades at school seem to have gone up, which can't be a bad thing."

Then another voice spoke in reply. Her father. "But at what cost? Are we to have a daughter that . . . just mechanically goes about what she needs to do but has no time for emotions and a social life?"

"I know. I don't understand it. She's completely changed since she came back from that Summer Camp."

"I don't think she ever went. She came back early—*without* James and we still haven't had an explanation."

"Oh God, what's going on? I just want my daughter back."

". . . Perhaps, we should think about . . . some counselling for her."

"And then have kids at school calling her a nut-case?"

"Counselling doesn't have that stigma anymore, Madeline."

Evie told Laura to turn it off. She'd heard enough.

Paulo realised eventually that the Captain was heading towards the beach. On the way, the Captain was still holding onto hopes and slim chances. He was always the optimist.

"My theory," he said, while on the run, "is that Evie escaped. I don't know how. But I believe she's done it, because you see, only the best people wind up as passengers of the Train you know."

Paulo felt his heart do a little humble leap of joy when the Captain said this.

". . . People who the Almighty has a plan for, so no, she *wasn't* eaten by a shark."

"So why are we heading to the sea?"

"The Train's parked there. Logic dictates that if Evie's out, then we should get out and re-join. *Then* come up with a plan to put a stop to all this *Sanctuary* nonsense.

Nonsense wasn't the word Paulo would have used. "But the powers behind the Sanctuary seem pretty impenetrable, Captain."

"Impenetrable's quite a strong word. We know the Train can get *in*. We just have to hope and pray that it can get out with just as much ease . . . oh no."

"What is it?"

"Up ahead. In front of the Train."

"I can't see the Train."

(Of course, the Captain had put on his clever 'Train-spotting' lenses, and Paulo didn't have any.)

"Well just up ahead then," replied the Captain. "A1's got here before us."

It wasn't A1 personally. It was a group of men—dressed in black—waiting. Standing in a tight group between them and their way out.

The Captain and Paulo hadn't stopped moving, contrary to what Paulo instinctively wanted to do. The Captain had instructed him to keep moving, but at an easy, natural walking pace. "Just to test a theory," he had said.

The small group of four men didn't move from their post and as the two were rounding up on one side of them, for a moment it looked as though they had tricked them into thinking they were merely Sanctuary residents, out for a stroll along the beach. But when they actually came close to passing them entirely, the men's heads rotated slowly so that their faces could follow them. Then their bodies turned and all at the same time, as if rehearsed, they started coming after them. The Captain and Paulo then made a run for it.

"What exactly was your theory?"

"That they were just robots and were only programmed to sense the presence of two *running* figures and to chase them down, but . . . well, it was only a theory . . . unfortunately."

The Train was ten metres away at the most but the men were right on their tail suddenly. And with their next step, the Captain was tackled from behind, tripped up off of his feet and he landed on his stomach. Paulo quickly tried to pull him up again, but then he was grabbed by another one of them and held tightly around the chest. His ribcage felt like it was being crushed. The Captain scrambled to his feet again and found himself face to face with one of them.

"Look, can we just talk about this like sensible, mature adults?"

Unexpectedly, the man punched him square in the jaw, which sent him stumbling backwards in surprise (and pain). Before he'd had the chance to steady himself again, the man was there, ready to deliver the second blow. But with a sweep of his left arm, he managed to block this one. And (even though there aren't many things the Captain hates more than violence), he had to fight back with a swing of his right arm, and he landed it right in the man's stomach. The man coughed and wheezed a little and in his vulnerable position, the Captain delivered a second punch to his head and he staggered back, nurturing his face for a second or two.

While this was happening, Paulo performed a skillful maneuver on the man who was holding him and brought him to the ground. Immediately one of the other men jumped into action and tried to hold him again but almost in the blink of an eye, Paulo raised his leg up and tripped him over. He rolled a couple of times and landed on some unsteady rocks, which bruised and pierced him and caused him to slide down the rocky slope to some even more rockier ground down by the shoreline. Within no time at all, the man who had been holding him first picked himself up off the ground and was coming straight towards Paulo again.

The forth man in black was coming towards the Captain while the other one was still nursing his face. And so when he re-positioned himself for attack, it was two against one. They both came for him and out the corner of his eye, he saw a long, white fold-out, plastic beach lounge and in a flash, he turned, picked it up and held it front of his body like a barrier. It was much heavier than he expected and when both men plummeted into it and collapsed on the ground, it became obvious that it was actually a metal one. Only one of them was able to recover from such a collision, and he looked straight into the Captain's eyes threateningly.

Paulo's opponent was coming nearer and nearer to him with a strong, clenched fist. The Captain's opponent raised up a strong arm, grabbed the beach lounge from him and threw it to the ground. Both of them raised their strongest arm in the air, ready to deliver their mightiest blow. The Captain and Paulo were back to back. At the last second, they both ducked down to dodge the fatal blow . . .

. . . And then heard two loud *thuds* above them. When they opened their eyes, they saw their opponents both lying, knocked out on the sandy, rocky ground. They looked at each other and then breathed out in relief—the Captain not exactly feeling proud that they'd just injured four men. He rolled up the sleeve of the one lying next to him and saw a patch stuck to his bicep. He peeled it off carefully and examined it. Just a square bit of clear, bluey-green plastic.

Then, as the two of them started to stand up, there was a strange scuttling noise all around them. Within seconds, it got louder and louder. They looked down and saw ten or twelve little metal objects crawling around on thin metal legs like spiders all around their feet.

"What the?" Paulo uttered, before one of them climbed onto his foot, and started crawling up his leg. "Ergh!" he exclaimed. "Get it off!"

But the Captain was busy with his own electronic creepy crawlies to worry about. There were now at least twenty of them all ganging up around them. More and more started crawling onto them, as though their purpose was to cover the runaways from head to toe. And again, no one around the place seemed to be paying any attention. No amount of calling for help was going to get them anywhere at all!

Chapter Fifteen

Introducing Mr. Cameron

The two girls were somber for a moment and then Laura said, "We've got to find a way of stopping this. My conscience would never leave me alone if I didn't try. And *then*, if that wasn't enough, we've somehow got to find a way of getting home and fixing our lives up."

Evie considered what Laura had said. "Getting home's the easy part," she said, thinking of the Train. (That is, if she would ever see it and the Captain again.) "But I can't imagine how we could do anything to stop someone like A1."

"Well that's where I have an idea. But first I need to find it."

"You need to *find* your *idea*? Huh?"

Laura left Evie's side and entered into the museum of glass boxes. Evie followed her a little way, but discovering it was like a maze and losing her on the first corner, made her decide to stay behind.

For Laura, there was a desperate face on the inside of every glass cell, pleading with her to let them out. Laura tried to convey to the first few she passed that she intended to free them, but not just yet. The more and more she passed however, she found it easier to try and ignore them, saying sorry to them in her own heart. She did however, have to glance at every one of those faces, because it was one particular face she was looking for.

Evie was beginning to wonder what had happened to Laura, when suddenly she could hear her footsteps again and she emerged from the silent crowd, but she hadn't come out alone.

A tall, ageing, tired looking man was with her. If his clothes were fresh and his hair was tidy he'd look very distinguished.

"This," said Laura, almost out of breath, "is my idea." Then she turned and looked up at him. "I'm sorry, I don't even know your name."

"Cameron," he said in a tired, but friendly voice. "Ben Cameron."

Laura looked back at Evie. "Mr. Cameron's Sanctuary code was A7, and you know what *that* means."

Evie started to shake her head, but then an idea flashed into her mind—*of course!* "He was the seventh person to live in the Sanctuary?"

"Seventh person registered, yeah. He was there when it all started. If anyone knows the ins and outs of the Sanctuary, it'd be him! Right?" The last word was aimed at Mr. Cameron.

"Well I know its foundations; its layout, its original purpose, the network; that sort of thing," said Mr. Cameron. He had a distinguished English accent, like A1.

"But, how come you're down here?" Evie asked. "As one of A1's collection? What happened?"

"I was part of a council," he coughed wrenchingly. "There were eight of us. A1, the head of course. We were the head of staff for a *luxury holiday resort establishment* called *The Sanctuary*. As the years went by, A1 was . . . changing. He was becoming twisted in his ideas about what the place should be—what it should be for. He made it so we didn't have names anymore but *codes*, and then he included the customers and soon, he didn't let people go. There's a long sordid story there about his mental health I believe," he coughed again into his hand. "But eventually we had to take a stand—those of us who thought it was terribly unethical. Old Cartwright and Filby passed away shortly after that—just of old age. The rest of them stuck by A1's side, remaining members of his staff—they're probably still up there working for him now. I couldn't understand how they could go along with what A1 was doing. Frightened for their lives perhaps. Or hungry for wealth. But I couldn't stand by and let it all happen. I knew what he was doing to people who wouldn't cooperate. I knew what he planned to do to fill the gap that was left behind in a person's life after they'd been trapped here. I did all I could to convince him it was wrong . . . and pointless—he didn't have much to gain from it. But I supposed his mind was corrupt with power and this insane obsession to *collect* people." He finished by coughing again. Laura assisted him by patting him on the back and stabling him.

She asked, "Do you want to sit down?"

But he refused, saying that he'd been doing nothing but sitting all the time in that horrible glass box. Laura agreed.

"In the end I showed too much opposition to his plans, and so he staged my death and sent me down here through some teleport device thing that he'd invented. Goodness knows what other frightful inventions he's created to serve his purposes while I've been down here."

"It was only by chance that I found out you existed down here, Mr. Cameron," said Laura. "When they came down here with one of the meals, they brought you out to have a word with you—mostly mocking you and giving you a hard time. But because they have to open the glass barriers enough to push some food through, I overheard enough to give me some hope that you might be able to help us defeat A1."

"Defeat A1?" Mr. Cameron said. His tone of voice utterly dashing all hopes that were welling up inside Laura and Evie.

"Well please tell me . . . that with your knowledge, and our . . . well our . . . don't take this the wrong way, but our fit, youthful bodies . . . that we could possibly have a chance at stopping him . . . and getting home."

A faint smile crept onto Mr. Cameron's lips. "Oh, I believe we might come up with some plans if we got talking. It was just the way you put it. *Defeat A1* . . . sounds like some kind of computer game."

The girls sighed in hopeful relief.

Although calling for help wouldn't get the Captain and Paulo anywhere, when they placed one foot in front of the other, this amazingly seemed to get them somewhere. It got them closer and closer to the shoreline of the beach.

"Just keep walking towards the water!" the Captain shouted, before one of the electronic critters crawled over his mouth and clamped it shut.

In a few seconds, there had been ideas flashing through the Captain's mind of how to disrupt the functioning of these little robots. He'd pictured all the gadgets he had sitting in his pockets and what use they might have been in a situation like this. None of them terrific and besides, each one of those plans involved him getting a hand *inside* one of his pockets, which may have proved impossible—due to the twenty or thirty mechanic little pests hinting strongly that they didn't want him doing so. But when he'd looked up in frustration, trying to breath in some fresh air without getting a metal leg in his throat, he saw the ocean. The simplest way to short-circuit some electronic wiring, was to get it wet. And there was plenty of *wet* available not twenty metres away!

Anyway, now Paulo and the Captain were dragging themselves across the rocks and across the sand, and as soon as one foot was placed into the salty swirling surf, the critters at their ankles fizzed, buzzed and then froze up, before dropping off into the water. Without hesitation, they both dived in, making sure the ones on their heads got a nice, cool swim too.

It had worked. They were free of them, and after high-fiving each other, they climbed out and quickly headed back to the Train—sopping wet.* The Captain got out the Train key, and just as he turned the key in the lock, Paulo saw something move out the corner his eye. "Did that bush just move?"

There was an eruption of laughter in A1's office—A1 seated in his big chair, leaning back comfortably staring up at the big screen on his wall as if watching a good movie on telly.

"What?" said the Captain.

---

* I'll just mention this now, in case you were wondering whether there was a flaw in the story—that the Captain's pockets were of course completely water-proof. They were lined, and just inside them were clever zips which he always made sure were zipped up when he was anywhere near water.

"I swear that bush behind us just moved."

"Don't swear, it's not nice." He stepped down, away from the Train's door and looked where Paulo was pointing. "Which bush?"

A round, thick prickle bush in front of them rolled a few centimetres towards them.

"*That* one!" said Paulo.

"How *very* interesting," said the Captain, stepping closer to try and examine it.

"Get back, Captain!" Paulo yelled as the bush rolled further. Then suddenly, as if in the blink of an eye, surrounding them were six or seven of the same bushes, rolling forwards of their own accord! And once again, before they could think quickly enough, there were two of the big prickle bushes in between them and their escape vehicle.

A1 was feeling very entertained. "Oh this is the funniest thing I've seen in ages! *Did that bush just move.* Ha ha! Very good!"

"Can't you stop them, Captain?"

"Er . . ." He plunged his hands inside his pockets, but it was too late—the bushes rolled right over them as if they had a mind of their own and the two were completely clobbered by them.

"Ouch, ooh, ooh, ow!" they were both exclaiming, while the force of the bushes brought them tumbling down onto the ground again and seemed to hold them there—immobile. This time, they couldn't even find the strength to drag themselves anywhere. It seemed that A1 had won. The ambushing, killer prickle bushes had done the trick.

A1 giggled in his chair and then sighed, while standing up finally. "Well, I suppose I'd better go and get them out of their little pickle." He turned off the big screen and the wall came gliding back over the top to conceal it again. "Or *prickle* in this case," he said on his way out, still chuckling to himself.

"So you really think we might have a chance?" Evie asked Mr Cameron.

"If we knock our heads together and be smart about it, I reckon we might."

"Knock our heads together? Is that really necessary?"

"That's an expression, young lady."

"Oh," Evie said, feeling her cheeks flush. "I knew that."

"But before we do anything," said Laura, "we really need to be out from under their power. We need to know how to get *out* of the Sanctuary—so that we know we have an escape-route at any time."

"Oh!" Evie exclaimed.

"What's wrong?"

"Nothing! But I just didn't realise until now that you wouldn't know!"

"Know *what*?"

"Well, I'm not one hundred percent sure . . . but maybe ninety-eight percent sure . . . that we're actually already outside the Sanctuary."

Laura's eyes changed. They grew wide, and twinkled with rapidly rising hopes. "Hold up, ninety-eight percent? What does that ninety-eight percent rest on?"

Evie bit her lip. ". . . A feeling . . . But a very strong feeling!"

"Or do you mean the *absence* of a feeling?" Mr. Cameron asked.

Evie locked eyes with him. "Yeah!" She nodded vigorously. "And I reckon if we just go up those steps, you'll see what I mean."

The three of them did so, agreeing that once they had accomplished their mission, they would come straight back here and rescue all the others trapped down there.

"Wow," Laura said when they reached the open air. "A real deep, dark forest."

"Exactly," said Mr. Cameron. "*Not* like the manufactured forests in the Sanctuary." He breathed in a long, deep breath of fresh air. "You're right, Evie. I do believe we're not in the Sanctuary anymore."

"Yeah but . . . wait. We need to start off *inside* the Sanctuary don't we?" said Laura. "If we're going to confront A1."

Evie rolled her eyes around, feeling just a tad pleased with herself that she had the answer to this one too. "Well . . . if we're *outside* the Sanctuary *now* . . . then I know a way to get back *into* the Sanctuary . . . If you'll just follow me . . ." And she led the way, leaving the other two guessing at her every move. She felt (with a little giggle to herself) a teensy weensy bit like the Captain for a short while.

Chapter Sixteen

A Jump To The Heart Beat

I don't know if you've ever been covered head to toe with prickle bush, but let me tell you, it's not a pleasant experience, as I'm sure you can imagine.

Paulo tried to wriggle out of it, but the only outcome of that was more and more prickles in his side and what seemed to be an even tighter grip on him. He knew the Captain was still right next to him. Would he be able to hear him? "I know that you always look for the most opportune moment, Captain, but . . . do you think maybe this might be a good time to use your Atom Relocating Molecular Teleport Device?"*

He did hear him. "I think you could have hit the nail on the head there, young friend."

He moved his arm in order to reach into his right trouser pocket—where he *knew* he had the device. This turned out to be a very difficult task because every move he made only led to more prickles in his side and what seemed to be an even tighter grip on him.

---

* One has to think very carefully before using an Atom Relocating Molecular Teleport Device because once used (just once), it takes twenty-four hours for it to fully charge up before it's ready to be used again.

At the same moment, A1 arrived at the beach and was walking towards the two pathetic piles of wriggling prickle bush. He stopped when they were at his feet. He took a brief moment to laugh out loud and then he ordered the bushes off of them. At his command, they tumbled clumsily away . . .

. . . And he was utterly baffled to see . . . Nothing but rocky sand beneath.

A1's smile disappeared. "But . . . but I saw them. I saw them get trapped . . . WHERE ARE THEY?" he roared, causing the little bushes to shrink further away into the undergrowth and he searched angrily in every nook and cranny along the beach. The Train, of course, he couldn't see and not being able to see it (because it was invisible to him and he couldn't see it) he walked straight into the side of it. And because he wasn't just walking, but walking with such a fiery, tempestuous rage, he knocked himself out. As luck would have it (even though that is a terrible thing to say) he got a good deal of solid sleep for the next little while.

The Captain and Paulo materialised in a new place—the Captain with a grip of Paulo's arm and both lying on the floor. They got up straight away, giving their limbs a stretch and scratching themselves all over from the irritating pins and needles feeling they had as a result of being covered in prickles.

Paulo looked around, confused at his surroundings. "Why didn't you make us materialise in the Train? That's where we were trying to get to before we were molested by soldiers, mechanical spiders and prickle bushes.

"I know, but that was before we were detained by the prickle bushes."

"Huh?"

They were right smack in the middle of A1's office, and without wasting any time, the Captain strode over to a wall, pressed the button that he remembered A1 had pressed, and part of the wall slid back to reveal the big screen. Without the Captain having to do anything else, it displayed the scene of the beach where they had just been seconds before.

They saw A1 there, his face getting redder and redder as he started out to search the beach.

"Just as I thought," the Captain said, with relief. "A1's gone down there to collect us." He looked at Paulo. "Only common sense."

"Yes but now he's discovered we're not there, he might come straight back here . . . to plan something else."

"He may well, so we don't have the place to ourselves for long."

They heard a *thump* suddenly and looked up at the screen.

"Oooh," said the Captain, cringing. "Nasty."

"Did you plan that?"

"Of course not. I can't help it if he doesn't watch where he's walking."

"But that's the Train he walked into. He probably *was* watching where he was going."

The Captain realised he still had his glasses on. "Oh, whoops. I forget sometimes."

"Well now that we're here, what shall we do?"

"Have a general snoop about, was my plan."

The Captain went straight for A1's desk to see what was there. From the front, it looked like just a desk—a large desk, free of mess and beautifully polished. It curved around to form almost a semi-circle of desk, as though it was engulfing the chair behind it in a kind of air-hug. When the Captain walked around *behind* the desk, he saw drawers and drawers and drawers—big wide, deep ones; about five across and three down. He opened one of the top ones and it slid out smoothly and silently. Now I don't know about you, but I find drawers interesting. Especially other people's drawers—if you ever get the chance to look in one without them catching you. Sometimes I think someone's drawer (or more accurately what's *in* the drawer) can tell you what kind of person they are. In light of this, I think you'll find the contents of A1's drawer quite interesting—as did the Captain.

As a controlling, manipulating type of person we know A1 to be by now, what would you expect to find in his drawer?

What else? . . . but controls. The drawer was filled with controls. Buttons and levers, knobs and switches. Lights and microphones, toggles and speakers. Every drawer was the same, and the Captain began to understand how A1 seemed to have eyes everywhere in the Sanctuary—how he could know *everything* that was going on. One drawer was for audio communication to and from the Infirmary. In another drawer, you could choose between listening to the sounds of the main village square and main streets, listening in on conversations in the restaurant kitchen, or a private conversation in someone's house where a hidden microphone had been placed. A number of drawers were dedicated to surveillance. There were rows of buttons all labelled: 'Sanctuary Café', 'Sanctuary Newsagent', 'Village Square: East", 'Village Square: North' (etcetera), and then 'Infirmary', under which was 'Halls', 'Beds', 'Waiting Rooms', 'Recovery Room', 'Patching Room', (etcetera). Up on the big screen on the wall opposite would appear live views of all these places instantly. In another drawer like these there were buttons labelled: 'External Psychiatry and Therapy Rooms'. All of these looked like ordinary consulting rooms you'd find in various different countries on various different planets—where people go to receive counselling and psychiatric care. In a drawer lower down there were two buttons labelled 'receive' and 'release' (whatever that meant) and underneath, buttons that turned out to be for the surveillance of what looked like the acres of land outside the Sanctuary—in the other dimension. So this was how A1 could see the Captain out there wandering around being completely deceived before he entered the Sanctuary. The Captain was about to try another button to see what would come up next, when suddenly there was some activity on the screen. There was another one of those wanderers—just like the Captain, only he was alone, walking around, enjoying the fresh air and the warm sunshine. The Captain didn't recognise him, but he recognised the signs of one being pulled subtly into the trap.

Paulo noticed the man on the screen. He knew it wouldn't do any good, but somehow, as an automatic reflex action he waved his hands in the air and yelled at the screen, "No! Don't! Get away from there! Go! You're gonna get . . ."

Suddenly, there came the light and the poor man was engulfed utterly by it. At the same moment, a signal lit up in the drawer the Captain was looking in and a gentle beeping sound filled the room. The light that was flashing on and off was also a small button, which was just at the Captain's index finger. He pressed it. And a computerised voice said, "*Attention needed of Sanctuary Resident A1. Potential Sanctuary visitor at outer inter-dimensional field.*

Temporarily held in time suspension beam. Please choose 'receive' or 'release'." Then there was a pause. It came again: "*Please choose 'receive' or release'."*

The Captain looked down at the buttons. *Receive.* Or *Release.* The Captain looked up at the man caught in the time suspension beam, then he looked back down at the buttons. He shrugged and pressed *Release.* The voice said: "*Are you sure? If so, press 'release'. If you made a mistake, press 'receive'."*

He pressed *release.*

"*Are you sure?"*

"Yes," he pressed it again.

"*Are you sure you want to complete this action?"*

"Yes!" he replied pressing it again.

That was the last time the voice spoke, and he quickly looked back up to the screen. The light melted away from the man. He stumbled a little bit, then shook his head and kept on walking—the strange luring properties in the air around the outskirts of the invisible Sanctuary no longer having an effect on him.

Paulo and the Captain looked at each other, looked back at the screen, and then back at each other again. Paulo let off an amazed one-syllable laugh, and the Captain sat down on A1's chair staring over all the controls in the open drawers. Almost in disbelief, the Captain said, "It's just like running a computer. The Sanctuary depends on the person who's controlling it!"

"Well that's profound," Paulo said with sarcasm.

"But it's not like the operation of it is set in motion and impossible to stop or at least very very difficult. The Sanctuary's just a giant computer that needs someone to tell it what to do."

Paulo looked blank.

"Don't you see what this means?" The Captain leaned back comfortably in the chair. His voice lowered significantly. "I have the power." He joined the fingertips of his right hand to the fingertips of his left hand. "I have hundreds and hundreds of people in my control while I sit in this chair. There is no free will. There is only *my* will because I have their strings wrapped around my little fingers and I possess the key to their souls. I could rule the world with this power. I could rise up as the most feared being in the entire galaxy and slowly gain control of it, star system by star system. Today the Sanctuary . . . tomorrow THE UNIVERSE!!!"

Paulo was frowning intensely. "Are you sure that's what it means, Captain?" he said with some fear.

He suddenly spoke in his normal voice and looked at Paulo like a friend again. "Well it could mean that for someone but for us it means we could actually stop A1, and it's going to be much simpler than I thought," he said with a broad smile.

"Now where is it? It can't be too far from here," said Evie, walking through the thick forest at lightening speed—the other two stumbling behind her, (partly because Laura was waiting for Mr. Cameron to catch up just about every ten seconds to help him across the rough uneven ground—he didn't have a lot of strength left in him). "We passed my tree earlier and I wasn't running all that far from that animal."

"Animal? There's animals out here?" said Laura worriedly.

"Hey, this looks familiar," Evie said, slowing down a little bit.

Because of the slowing down, Mr. Cameron had a chance to catch up again. "It certainly *does* look familiar."

"You recognise this place?" asked Evie.

"If I'm not mistaken, then I not only recognise it, I helped design it."

"You designed a forest?" asked Laura. "But it looks so . . . natural."

"No, no. I helped design . . ."

"The portal?" asked Evie, suddenly realizing what he could possibly be talking about.

He spoke between gasps for breath for he was still a little puffed out. "Yes. I gather . . . that was how you came to be here, young Evie."

She nodded.

"Yes it was created . . . er to be an emergency exit."

"An emergency exit?" asked Laura, hardly believing it.

"Yes. For emergencies. And . . . it's basically . . . a doorway to another dimension. A dimension . . . er where the Sanctuary lies. And er . . . ah, there's a familiar tree."

"That's it!" shouted Evie.

They all arrived and stopped right in front of the tree with the big hole in its trunk. The three just stood there for a while—hesitating.

Nervously, Laura said, "Well come on. What are we waiting for? This is what we set out to do isn't it?"

"Yes," said Evie. "But it's the thought of stepping back into the Sanctuary. Where we know how it feels to be utterly trapped."

"And paralysed."

"And frustrated."

"We must though," said Mr. Cameron, making a move towards the tree. "Give me a booster will you?"

They helped the fragile Mr. Cameron up into the hole in the tree. The two girls followed and Laura was amazed to suddenly find herself popping up out of the ground and having to climb up onto land—when she was sure she'd just entered vertically.

"This forest looks so different," she said after steadying herself on her feet. "So . . . kept and friendly-looking."

"Give me the other forest any day," said Evie, and Laura smiled and nodded in reply.

Then Mr. Cameron spoke. "Now, here, in the Sanctuary, we're technically dead so unless we make a scene and draw attention to ourselves everywhere we go, we *should* go unnoticed. Just try and blend in, and we should be alright. Remember, there's surveillance cameras hidden about the place. The safest thing is to pretend they're absolutely everywhere . . . I wouldn't be surprised if there were by now—goodness *knows* how long I've been down in that place."

"So where do we go from here?" asked Laura.

Before Mr. Cameron answered, Evie spoke, "I reckon we just head for that big place of A1's."

"But *then* what? Do we have a plan?"

"I don't know what it is, but I just really feel that we should go there. Plan or no plan." Evie had no idea why she was saying this, but every word of it was true. It's how she did feel, deep down. Maybe it was that *woman's intuition* that her mum talked about sometimes . . . was *fourteen* old enough to have *woman's* intuition? Or maybe it wasn't her mum's strange phenomena coming into play but her Pastor's. That whole *being led by God* thing. If so, it would be an actual answer to an actual prayer. It was something she'd mentioned to God that night in the tree trunk. *Oh yes, and a way out of this mess would help too, God . . . please . . .*

Well, it was the only feeling she had, so she stuck with it. And the other two seemed to just go with it too. Obviously there was no plan they had of their own, so any decision made by anyone was terrific. So the three of them looked for the quickest way out of the forest and straight into the heart beat of the Sanctuary.

"This is amazing!" said Paulo. "There's no button anywhere that says *release everybody from the Sanctuary* is there?"

"Unfortunately not."

"How about *Take all power away from A1?*"

"U-uh. Ooh, have a look at this," said the Captain, after pressing one of the buttons in the 'External Psychiatry and Therapy Rooms' drawer.

Up on the screen was a scene of a consulting room as before, but this time, somebody was in there with the consultant, speaking to them and fidgeting in the chair, while the consultant (who'd called herself Sue) nodded and said "I see" a lot. Eventually, the client had broken down into tears and the consultant said, "I see. Why don't you come this way, I've got just the remedy for you."

The Captain and Paulo watched the consultant take the client into a little side room and they disappeared through the door. The Captain looked down at the control panel to see if he could get a picture of them beyond the door. He pressed a button very near which said 'Transition Room' and then they were suddenly looking at a tight little room with a small platform in the centre which the client was being placed on and then a large glass barrier like a box came down around her. 'Sue' pressed a button above the platform and suddenly there was an alert signal in A1's office again.

Attention needed of Sanctuary Resident A1. Potential Sanctuary visitor in consulting room on Planet Jaxox. Transition to Sanctuary confirmation needed. Please choose 'receive' or 'reject'.

"Reject it! Reject it!" said Paulo.

"I was going to," said the Captain. With a smile and a lick of his lips, he pressed the button that was labelled 'reject'. After several questions asking whether the Captain was *sure* he absolutely wanted to, on the screen, the client was released by Sue and by the looks of it, was allowed to go home.

They laughed and the Captain suddenly came across another section of the control panel labelled 'Sue and Mark control bank'. He pressed a random button and on the screen came the words 'ARE YOU SURE YOU WANT TO SHUT DOWN THIS 'SUE' UNIT?'

. . . And the Captain pressed 'yes' and the consultant woman keeled over, slowly bending from the waist and letting her arms droop—just like a wind-up toy that's wound down.

They laughed again in astonishment.

"Having fun?" said a voice from the doorway. It wasn't Paulo's. It wasn't the Captain's. It didn't even belong to the tiny imp that lived inside the Captain's breast pocket. It was A1, and he was standing just inside the room with one tough looking man dressed in black at either side of him.

"Er, yes actually," replied the Captain, taking a small bottle of some kind of juicy drink out of his pocket and drinking it.

"We should have kept an eye on the beach, Captain," Paulo said, sidling across the room to stand next to the Captain.

"Yes, well I don't know whether this screen has pip-action," he muttered back.

"I'm sure I don't have to remind you that this is *my* private office," said A1, coming further into the room slowly.

"No no no, of course not. I was actually just admiring this desk of yours. All these controls!" The Captain pushed drawers in and pulled drawers out and pressed all sorts of buttons while he was talking. "May I just say, what an amazing set up you've got here." Just then, the Captain *stopped* pressing buttons as he shot a passing glance at that big screen in the wall. Without letting it show on his face, he got a BIG surprise. Paulo saw it too. It was Evie on the screen, in the main square of the Sanctuary with two other people, walking around cautiously, trying not to be noticed.

"I suppose you want me to explain to you how it all works." A1's body was rotating around slowly to face the screen.

The Captain quickly interjected, "Ah, no, not really!" And he quickly pushed another button to get the screen to display something else. "I think that might spoil all the magic for me. It's all rather impressive, but to put it plainly I think you could make a few improvements."

"Oh really? Well to put it *plainly* for you, A7 . . . I'm not interested. I don't know how you got out of the prickle bushes, but you're beginning to make me quite angry."

"Oh really? Well I rather see that as a good sign." While talking, the Captain and Paulo were backing away slowly, shoulder to shoulder. But what they didn't realise is that the two men dressed in black had edged their way around them and were now waiting right behind them. "That was just what I was going for," continued the Captain. "You see, because not only does anger make people dangerous, it can make them a little bit careless as well, did you know that?"

With a huge, amused smile, A1 replied, "No I didn't know that. But tell me A7, who were you suggesting was the careless one?"

Just then, both the Captain and Paulo felt an extremely strange feeling on their arms and within seconds, they were in the arms of the two men dressed in black. They immediately felt so light-headed, they couldn't stand up anymore and they collapsed right into the mens' waiting arms. The Captain, seeing the patch that had just been slapped onto his arm, said woozily, "Ah, me I suppose," before he and Paulo completely lost consciousness.

Chapter Seventeen

Handy Solutions

A couple of minutes later, when the Captain could hear that the men had left the room, he opened his eyes and looked around. He was lying on a metal bed on wheels in a round laboratory. Paulo was on another bed next to him, unconscious. "Lucky I drank some of my Temporary Toxin Neutralising Solution," he said to himself as he got up from the bed, took the patch off his arm and crinkled it up to throw away. He leant over Paulo and gently lifted his eyelids, the way a doctor would. "As I thought. The boy with kaleidoscope eyes. That patch must really be powerful. Looks like it was just a sleeping-aid though, luckily." He looked down at the patch on Paulo's arm. Taking it off would probably bring him back to consciousness, but he thought there would be no harm in leaving him there for a while to rest. "Now," he said, clapping his hands together, eyes shining. "What damage can I do down here?"

He noticed first of all, a cabinet on one side of the lab with lots of small boxes of patches all stacked up and ready to use. They were labelled—different strengths, different purposes. Some were just plain pieces of sticky plastic by the look of them. The Captain thought of destroying the contents of the whole cabinet—no more patches. But he knew they'd have many more boxes stocked up somewhere; this surely couldn't be all of them.

Then he saw a fire extinguisher hooked up close by. He could set fire to the place with his Manuel Hand Operating Fuel-Injected Flame Combustion Apparatus. The whole place would have to be evacuated and he could take control. But then it occurred to him that they might not be able to get out of there themselves. It would get rid of a problem alright—A1's problem. Himself and Paulo.

These plans did have a chance, he thought, but he was still hanging out for *the* plan. The one that was the quickest, the safest and the surest way of doing the job.

He rested for a bit, slumping against the wall and giving his neck a rub. No more ideas were coming and he felt useless for a tiny second down there in that laboratory, which, for a reasonably intelligent science-nut like the Captain, was a very rare thing. "My brain's fused out by the looks of it. I'm fresh out of ideas—that's me done! I can't do anymore by myself. I need you. Like I always do. What's something I can do?" He felt tired all of a sudden and out of steam. And just then, he heard commotion outside and he had to think quick. He could either lie back down and pretend to be asleep still, or . . .

There was a rack near the door with doctor's coats hanging on it.* He rushed over and put it on, feeling a sudden rush of hot fury when his arm wouldn't go through one of the arm holes because the person before him hadn't put it completely back through the right way.

There were voices right outside the door, and just in time, the Captain, in his white coat and last minute

---

*   Great minds think alike.

addition of a pair of glasses, stood at the head of Paulo's bed appearing as though he was performing a check-up on him.

Two young ladies who obviously didn't expect someone to already be in the room, stopped in the doorway.

"Come in," said the Captain, "come in. You're not interrupting anything. Just making sure this one's not going to wake up for a while."

They stepped in further. One of them said, "There's a top-up scheduled for now. Is the lab free?"

"Yes, yes! By all means."

The two girls, (who looked like nurses) came in, followed by a long line of men dressed in black. The Captain frowned in curiosity and wheeled Paulo out of the way.

"What exactly are you doing?" he hesitated to say.

"We told you, a top-up. We've got to give these workers another fresh patch or they'll turn on us. They don't all work for A1 of their own free will, remember?"

"Yes, of course, well . . . er, let me help you."

"That would be good actually. Sometimes it's hard to keep them all still."

"Well you two do that. I'll get the patches." He didn't know exactly what he was going to do yet, but surely, he was in an opportune position.

"Don't forget to wash your hands before and after," one of the nurses said. "The solution to soak them in is over there."

Thank you, thought the Captain. *I just got the idea I was waiting for!* He was in charge of soaking the patches in the very solution that caused temporary loss of self control and free-will. He went over to the bench where it all was, and while always keeping one eye on those nurses, he removed the necessary amount of patches from the boxes and carried them and the tub of solution over to the sink. He also found a similar tub which was empty, and carried that over as well.

He ran the water in the sink to wash his hands, holding the identical tub underneath the tap, filling it up. Instead of soaking the patches in the solution, he soaked them, bold as anything, in the tub of water. The nurses didn't so much as glance over, which was good, for obvious reasons.

"Now ladies," said the Captain, "a quick test for you. How long must you soak the patches for?"

One of them smiled, and replied immediately, "Between two and three minutes."

This is too easy, thought the Captain. "Very good," he said, and watched the second hand on his watch tick slowly around a couple of times. When it had gone about nine seconds after two minutes, the Captain took them out one by one and handed them to one of the nurses, and from then, it was like a well-rehearsed production line. The Captain would hand one to the first nurse, she would place it on the upper arm of a groggy man dressed in black, then the other nurse would take him quickly out the door, across the hall and into another small room opposite—a holding bay for when they were ready to be used. The Captain paid close attention to where this room was and how to get in and out of it.

By the end of the progression, there were about fifteen or twenty men all stocked up in that room, and the nurses politely went away leaving the 'doctor' to carry on looking after his 'patient'. This time of course, the door was not locked behind them—the nurses had been innocent mutineers.

When he was sure they were gone, the Captain was onto Paulo, trying to wake him up before *their* nurses or doctors came to 'look after' them.

"Well, that's A1's place there. That's where he lives, where he works and where he takes a holiday. All the controls for the Sanctuary, *everything* . . . is in there." Mr. Cameron was pointing towards the big, round, concrete building beyond the high fences and the pretty path, and underneath the hanging gardens.

They were casually sitting at a table outside a café, with tropical drinks with tiny umbrellas sitting in the top.

"I wondered what that building was, right next to the Infirmary," said Evie.

"You never went in there?" asked Laura.

"Nup. What's it like?"

Laura shrugged. "Just as dull as the Infirmary. They're more or less the same building."

"Huh?"

"They connect underground," explained Mr. Cameron. "Fairly practical when you think of it."

"Well it's very impressive," said Evie, "but how do we get in? Look at those huge gates! And the surveillance cameras all around!"

"Well I don't know, but there's a chance the security code at the gate will still be the same as it was when I was working here. All the council members knew it."

"It's a pretty slim chance isn't it?" Laura said, doubtfully.

Mr. Cameron gave a serious nod of the head. "Very slim indeed."

The Captain's plan was to escape, as it so often is. But there was a snare. Just as Paulo had finally started to be able to walk on his own two feet again without needing a prod in the side from the Captain to wake him up every ten seconds, they heard noises outside again.

"What did he want us to do again?" asked one doctor.

"Just bring 'em up to the boss and that's it."

"Why does he need a couple of doctors to do that?"

"I don't know. He just said there'll be a man and a younger lad on beds fast asleep and we have to wheel them up to him, that's all. I don't ask questions. Here we are."

He pulled down on the door handle with a key card in his other hand at the ready. But the handle went down freely and released the latch.

"I thought you said he said this would be locked."

"I did. And he did."

"You daft ape. You probably can't take down a message properly."

"I'm sure that's what he said."

"I'm not trusting *you* again to pass on a message. Look, there they are. Come on. You take one, I'll take the other."

The Captain and Paulo were lying back down on the beds and the doctors assumed them to be unconscious. They wheeled them out into the hallway.

"What he *might* have said, *Master Mind*, was to lock the door *after* we've got 'em."

"He might have, yeah."

"Well there you are then. I'll lock it, shall I?"

"Yeah, go on then."

The Captain and Paulo dared not open their eyes to see where they were, incase one of them saw them. They could feel that they were going around corners, this way and that, then into a lift and taken up, but they lost all sense of direction—even though the Captain was quite good at that. They could make a good guess though at who *the boss* was, and therefore where they would be taken.

Soon, they could feel a different, cooler temperature come over them—an air-conditioned room—wide and spacious. And a new voice in the mix, but well known to them straight away.

"Ah, thank you very much. You didn't have any trouble from them on the way up?"

"No A1, they're still sleeping."

"Right you can go now. I shan't want any witnesses."

That doesn't sound good, thought Paulo. What didn't he want witnesses *for*?

"Now my two dear trouble-makers," said A1 after the two dozy doctors had left the room. "I would have come down to you in that lab, but I thought it more fitting that you should be up here in this office that you seemed to find so interesting—for your last moments of life. Yes, you may be surprised. I did very much want you as one of my prized collection pieces. You A7, not C36, you don't matter so much. But it will be such a shame to lose you; to lose anyone come to that. But I'm afraid when a resident of the Sanctuary becomes volatile, I have no other choice but to retire them . . . to the Sanctuary Underground." He laughed, "But I can't even send you down there because you're so clever, you'll probably come up with some clever way of escaping!"

Paulo was itching to say, "So why can't you just let us go then?" But he couldn't. He might disturb the plan that he hoped the Captain had.

"In this case," continued A1, "I can actually say it will hurt me more than it hurts you. In fact, it'll be perfectly painless for you both. But I'm losing my prized collection piece. Anyway, now that I've got you alone, and in a position where you're not going to cause some unwanted and very tiring disruption, I'm going to have to get rid of you; and get rid of the threat that you both pose to my special little way of life here, which, did I mention, is my life's work. It's a shame you won't be conscious for it. It'll be quite a significant moment, although quite simple. And also because I always find 'famous last words' very interesting indeed."

Paulo was panicking, his whole body burning with impatience—to sit up and defend himself. Any moment surely, he could cease to exist. Any breath he took could be his last. And he was wondering when the Captain would make a move! He'd always found it was in his best interest to trust the Captain, but as every second went by, he was losing another tiny ounce of faith.

Paulo and the Captain of course couldn't see anything, but if you were looking on from a short distance away, you would have seen A1 holding two large patches—one in each hand. What you wouldn't have seen though, was that the patches he was bringing nearer and nearer to the vulnerable pair were known as 'death' patches. Patches soaked in strong fatal poison.

There are other things you *would* have seen, such as a small plan the Captain had tucked away in his hand. He was clutching a small metal paper weight he'd found in the lab. If he and Paulo simply sat up and said "Ha HA! We're not actually unconscious, we're really awake and listening to everything you're saying!"—where would that get them? No, he had to distract him first. And a paper weight was going to do it.

He wriggled it carefully out of the well of his palm to the tips of his fingers, and then when A1's voice for a split second went quieter, presuming he'd turned his face toward Paulo, he launched the paperweight across the room and it made a sound at the far side of A1's big desk.

"And when you're good and dead," A1 went on, "I'll say there was a tragic accident and that's where I can use my imagination. Perhaps C36, you'll have gotten yourself mauled by one of those vicious bears in the forest that I keep telling everyone exist. Totally eaten up in one big mouthful. And A7 . . . perhaps you'll die from a terrible disease contracted by . . . ooh, I know, a rare type of plant, a prickle bush found near the beach which I'll heroically dispose of. Now, there must be no trace of a body, er . . . I know, you were so sick, you became delirious and wandered around in the desert and there was no trace of you ever since. How does that sound. Yes, I thought so too. Magnificent."

The Captain, expressionless, was devastated. The paper weight plan had not worked. A1 had not even heard it. And now he had no reason to hesitate any longer. He'd had his speech, enjoyed the moment of the impending death of his enemies, and was now determined to do the deed before anything could inconveniently interrupt!

Chapter Eighteen

The Battle Of The Captives

The Captain's last hope was the plan he thought wouldn't work very well—open their eyes at the last moment and hope that that takes him by surprise and distract him enough to prize the patches from his hand. But A1 was closer than the Captain thought. The patch was less than a millimetre away from the Captain's skin; he even felt it touch a hair on his arm. And just then, his plan B, (or G or H or whatever it was by now) went wrong, as a loud voice interrupted instead.

"No!!!" Whoever had yelled out was just peeping through a doorway which was slowly opening.

"How did you get in here?" A1 barked.

The Captain and Paulo opened their eyes and sat up in one single action. "Evie!" they exclaimed in unison.

A1 was quick to act. He called for some of his workers by pressing a few buttons. But it didn't seem to work.

"Looks like we got here just in time," said Laura, coming through the door after Evie.

"Come on!" A1 exclaimed, trying the buttons again for his workers to come to his aid.

"They won't come, A1," said the Captain. "I think you'll find they've grown tired of answering to your beck and call every five minutes."

"What have you done?"

"It's something to do with two different buckets, one with special solution in it and one with just water in it looking very similar. The nurses down there must have got them mixed up."

"How did *you* get in here?" he said again to Evie and Laura.

Then there was a third party that came through the door and A1 froze with astonishment. "A7," he said with dread.

"The name's Ben Cameron. It's always been Ben Cameron and it always will be Ben Cameron."

"As long as you're in the Sanctuary, you're A7,' A1 said bitterly. "And it's obvious we can't have two A7s at once."

"Careful Captain!" Evie yelled.

The Captain had been looking at the other A7, when from behind him, A1 was coming near again with the poison patch.

Luckily Evie had given him enough warning. He managed to snatch up A1's arm with his right hand and he twisted it until the patch dropped to the floor. A1 then gave up on this particular tact and stormed up closer to Mr. Cameron.

"Go on then. How did you get out of the underground?"

"You're a relatively clever man, A1. You can work it out."

While A1's attention was elsewhere, the Captain was whispering something to Paulo and soon after that, Paulo was looking for a discreet way out of the room.

"I assume this one had something to do with it," A1 said, referring to Evie.

Evie felt like pointing out that she in fact had a name too, but she was too afraid.

"What are you *doing* here, anyway," A1 continued, speaking to Mr. Cameron.

"I came here to try and reason with you. To see if I could persuade you to stop all this nonsense of keeping people here against their will."

"They're happy."

"Maybe *now* they are. But you take away those patches, give them their minds back and most of them would be demanding the way out in no time."

"That doesn't give me much incentive to give them back their free will then does it."

"But these are people's lives!

"This is my collection! My collection is my life!"

"Can anyone really be that selfish?"

"Obviously they can. You will never persuade me to willingly give up my life's work."

Laura then said, more so to Mr. Cameron, "Why don't we just grab 'im, you know, kind of house arrest?"

A1 lurched forward, quick as lightening, grabbed Laura (who'd probably made a mistake by speaking), and held her by his side, holding the poison patch that was intended for Paulo to her arm.

"Because, my dear," A1 said to Laura in reply, "if anyone tries to, you die. It's very simple.

"He's bluffing," Laura said after a short pause. "A bit of poison on a patch isn't gonna kill me instantly."

"Care to try it out?" said A1.

Everyone was still and looked unsure, except for A1 and Mr. Cameron. "I'm afraid it could kill you quite instantly young Laura," said Mr. Cameron, defeated. "I have no doubt that A1 could have invented something as ghastly as that."

"Oh, 7B12," said A1. "What a pity it would be if I had to use this on you. We've developed quite an interesting relationship over the years haven't we? Never been a dull moment yet. I was even quite sad to send you to the Sanctuary Underground. Having you here gave me something to do throughout the day. You always kept me on my toes."

"If I could, I'd put you on your back. Permanently!"

"Now Laura," said Mr. Cameron. "You don't wish to be a killer yourself do you?"

She sighed and hung her head. "No."

"May I just . . . put a word or two in here," said the Captain, getting their attention suddenly. He was quite calm and relaxed all of a sudden. Even light-hearted could be a word to describe him at this point. "It was very noble of Mr. Cameron to come here and try and solve things by talking, I must say. I really admire that. That's the way I like to do it, only it doesn't look like it's ever going to work this time. Clearly A1's never going to give up what he's got here, so Mr. Cameron, I think we ought to just, maybe give up trying."

"What?" Mr. Cameron said. "Which side are you on?"

"I think A1 should get what he deserves, you know, he's worked hard for this. I bet there's been a lot of blood, sweat and tears gone into developing this place, am I right?" The Captain had wandered over to him and he now patted him on the shoulder.

A1 nodded, but he was extremely suspicious.

The Captain continued. "You asked me whose side I'm on. Well actually, I'm on the side of A1's workers really. They do a *smashing* job. And while they do it, *quickly* and *efficiently*, using much *strength and persistence*, A1 gets exactly what he's asked for. Right Paulo?"

"Right," said Paulo, emerging from the double doors opposite the entrance door and letting a stream of A1's workers into the room—all with hammers, steel rods or broken off chair legs in their hands rampaging through A1's office heading straight for all the delicate equipment all laid bare around them.

The Captain was watching extremely carefully, for one second that A1 lost attention on Laura. When he did, the Captain yanked her away from him and took her, Evie and Mr. Cameron to safety in a corner of the room.

In no time at all, there were sparks flying, bits of equipment chipping up into the air, alarms going off, and A1's terrible, devastated voice crying out: "No! No! No! No! No! What are you doing? No!!!"

"This is what happens when you give people their free will and help them realise they've been kept as puppet slaves for a good part of their lives!" the Captain shouted over all the noise.

"Stop it! Stop it! I order you!" A1 was saying, pulling some of his ex-workers away from the controls. "You're destroying it! You're destroying everything!!"

"That's the general idea," said the Captain, who had his arms folded, leaning back on a wall, watching the progress.

With fervent anger firing in his eyes, A1 stormed over to him. But then, instead of going for the Captain, A1 went to a control that hadn't been destroyed yet. Another call for his workers.

"These aren't all of them Captain," he said.

"I'm aware of that," he replied with a slightly worried, yet still calm expression.

"The other troupe's patches won't have expired yet."

And in came a small army of more workers. Men dressed exactly the same as the Captain's small army, but this lot were behaving under the influence of the patch.

All of a sudden, a war had broken out, between A1's workers and A1's ex-workers and the Captain quickly commanded the others to get out of the room. With all the commotion, he couldn't actually see Evie, Laura, Paulo and Mr Cameron anymore. Perhaps most of them had already gotten out of there.

When an ex-worker wasn't being fought by a worker, he would carry on smashing up anything in sight with a passion, but a lot of the time, they were forced to defend themselves against the workers.

Soon, the Captain couldn't even see A1 anymore. The room was a cloud of fighting, struggling, wrestling and tug-of-war. The Captain tried to wade his way through it all to look for him—make sure he wasn't up to anything, but couldn't find him anywhere. He jumped over a wire flying across the floor and closely escaped a blow on the head with a hammer. He ducked when a circuit board came flying and skillfully dodged a stumbling ex-worker. Then one bumped into him from behind and thinking he needed to fight him, the worker swung a chair leg at the Captain. It brushed the top of his head before he grabbed it from him, tossed it down to the floor and then quickly decided he should get out of the firing line. He hopped, skipped and jumped it out of the room to where

Mr. Cameron, Laura and Paulo were crouching—just outside the doorway.

Something immediately struck him.* "Where's Evie?" he said.

"We thought she was with you," said Laura.

There was a pause. "I've got to go in and find her."

"No," said Mr. Cameron. "It's no good having one of us injured, and you surely will be if you go back in there."

"But Evie could be seriously injured already," said Paulo.

They watched the battle. It was hard to watch, but hard to look away. But good things were happening elsewhere as the fighting went on.

Consultants named Sue and Mark everywhere were winding down like flat batteries. Surveillance cameras were shutting down all over the Sanctuary, leaving people to their own privacy. Android imposters right across the galaxy were shutting down or mysteriously disappearing without trace.

Evie's mum was trying to talk some sense into her daughter. "Evelyn Bamford, you'd better be listening to me. This isn't just about you, this is about your whole family. Others are affected by your behaviour too, you know! That's why we're thinking . . . Evelyn? . . . Evie? What's happened? Paul!!!" . . . "What is it?" . . . "Something weird, I don't know . . . something's happened to her . . . oh . . ." and they proceeded to realise eventually that it had not been their daughter at all.♦

---

* Not a chair leg this time, an urgent thought—striking his mind.

♦ I have no record of what Madeline and Paul Bamford did after that. I expect there was much confusion and discussion

"Sounds as if things are cooling off in there now anyway," said Laura, after they'd been watching for a while.

She was right. There was still some fighting going on, but a lot of men were down and now the sides seemed to be much more uneven than before.

"Who's winning?" asked Mr. Cameron.

"I can't tell. They all look the same," said Paulo.

"You were with them when you brought them up from that room," said the Captain. "Don't you recognise at least one of them?"

"It's hard to see . . ."

Now there were eight or nine men onto just two.

"That one I recognise."

"Which?"

". . . The one on the floor . . . unconscious."

"That's not a good sign."

Just then, the fighting stopped, as the two men who seemed to be the ones in minority, dropped and the ones still left standing seemed to be satisfied and stopped fighting. I think the onlookers all stopped breathing for a few seconds as they still wondered which side had won. Until one of them looked straight at Paulo and smiled a tired, hearty smile—although not a happy one. Paulo stood and walked back into the room slowly and as he came nearer, he recognised the man. He had no patch

---

about what to *do* with this weird electronic facsimile of their daughter. I don't know what they did with it; whether they threw it in the bin, or took it to an electronics shop, hoping they would know what to do with it, or for all I know, they may have re-programmed it to do the dishes every night for them. However I *do* know that neither of them had much know-how in electronics and computer programming so this is unlikely.

on his arm and his face showed relief, triumph and also gratefulness.

"We had no idea we were doing all this work for A1. If we'd have realised, be assured, we wouldn't have helped him."

"We know," said the Captain, also entering after Paulo. "We know. Don't worry." He was pre-occupied though—looking for Evie.

"I don't like what we've just done," said another ex-worker.

"But it was necessary," said yet another. "Otherwise A1 would still have control over us. We have no time to waste though. We'd better see if these guys on the floor will be okay."

"Good idea," said the Captain. "The ones with patches . . . take them off. Help them up too."

Paulo, now having had a chance to assess the situation, said, rather disbelievingly, "Well . . . I think we've done it, Captain."

"You'll *never* win, Captain!" came a bitter voice from somewhere.

They all looked for A1, for they knew it was his voice. There was smoke floating around much of the room and a spark here and there from parts of computers short-circuiting. But in one area of A1's office, the smoke began to clear and they all saw A1, standing next to a large glass box—about the size of a telephone booth. The Captain was sure he'd seen one like it before recently, but couldn't quite remember where. But at the moment, he wasn't too concerned about this. It was what was inside the box—or to be more precise . . . *who* was inside.

"It's over, A1," said Mr. Cameron. "You have to give up now."

"But it's not. I can re-build all this in no time," he continued, looking almost like a maniac. "I did it once, I can do it again. Now if you'll just all leave the Sanctuary, I won't harm your friend here. I'm sorry I only know her as D14 the former."

"What do you mean by harm her?" said the Captain, very very angry and a little bit worried.

He laughed insanely. "This is a disintegrator, don't you know anything?"

Of course it was Evie in the box and when A1 said this, she gulped uncontrollably and almost lost her breath with fear. She had no control over her emotions. Everything was showing on her face, and tears rolled one after the other down her cheeks.

A1 smiled when he saw that the Captain's emotions were laid bare as well. He had hit his weakness—that he had a terrible conscience and couldn't let anyone die if he could help it.

The Captain couldn't let Evelyn die. What about her parents and her brother James? They would never know what'd happened to her. And she was such a precious girl. Not only in the Captain's eyes but in the Almighty's eyes. He believed that God must still have amazing plans for this girl. Her life couldn't end here. Did she even know Jesus well enough? Would he see her in heaven one day? All these thoughts were whizzing around in the Captain's head—in the background. But what was prominent in his mind was . . . *What on earth am I going to do?*

Evie suddenly spoke, making the Captain and the other's jump. All hope had gone from her face. Even though she was speaking through her tears, what she had to say was still very clear and steady. "You can't leave the Sanctuary now like he says, Captain. He'll continue this place just like he's been doing and all those people will still be trapped here. Lots of people will live like dirt in the Underground like they've been doing, and lots of people will die like they've been doing. Nothing will change. Don't trade all their lives in for mine, you can't do that. I'm just one person. There's thousands out there. You've got to stop A1, and save them."

"Oh do be quiet D14," A1 growled. "Your voice is irritating."

The Captain then, was speechless. This girl, this fourteen year old girl had just sacrificed her life for thousands of other people she didn't know. It's easy to say that isn't it. But would you actually do that?

Out the corner of his eye, the Captain could see Laura's face. And she seemed to be trying to get his attention.

"Well Captain," shouted A1, "won't you be on your way? I believe the original A7 can show you out of here. I think I'm ready to sacrifice a few interesting specimens like yourselves. Just get out."

The Captain finally glanced at Laura's face, and shock of all shocks, she was smiling. She also arranged her eyebrows into a particular shape that said something in particular. And the Captain remembered where he'd seen a similar glass box before.

"Oh how very big of you," said the Captain, looking back up at A1. "What a sacrifice. When you've heard what this young lady just said. You have not even a speck of decency or morality in comparison to this girl, so don't even utter the word sacrifice if you're talking about yourself. But . . ." he glanced down at Laura and then back up again, "I'm afraid we have no choice. 'No' is the answer to your question. We will not be leaving. Not until we know that you will never again be in control of this so-called Sanctuary. Do what you like. We're not giving up. Not today, thank you."

There was a look of horror on Evie's face as she clasped her hands together and looked up to heaven, before, in the blink of an eye, A1, with no remorse, pressed the button on the side of the box and a light came down upon her and zapped her out of existence. "If that's the way you want it. Then so it must be."

"No!!!" cried Mr. Cameron immediately, running over towards A1. "You monster! How could you do tha . . ." he was face to face with him. Then he slowly nodded and looked at A1 as though he was a piece of rotting fruit covered in ants and flies and stinking to high-heaven. "Because you're who you are. You're a black-hearted, inhuman, monstrous, calloused, crook!" As he was describing him, he felt more and more passionate about what he was saying and he opened the glass box and shoved A1 inside.

A1 just chuckled. "Why not? I've not much to live for now." Then he laughed and laughed and laughed until Mr. Cameron pressed the disintegration button and he was gone. To where Evie had gone?

Chapter Nineteen

Welcome Aboard

"Well *that* should get rid of him for a while," said Laura, hardly being able to suppress a smile.

Mr. Cameron's expression changed from sadness and anger, to a gaping frown. "For a *while*?"

Laura stuttered a little and her face also changed. "W-what? You didn't know?"

"Didn't know what?"

"Captain you seem awfully relaxed as well," said Paulo with a pleading face, "what's going on here?"

The Captain merely looked to Laura for explanations. Laura smiled—big this time, and said, "Follow me and I'll show you."

As they left the room after Laura, the Captain said, looking at the casualties in the room, "Er . . . you'd better er . . ."

One of the ex-workers finished, ". . . get them to the Infirmary. Will do!"

"Good, well done," the Captain said hurriedly, and then he was gone. For a change, he was the one at the back of the pack. It was Laura up front, then Paulo, then Mr. Cameron, and then the Captain.

It was another good afternoon's walk to that beautiful, organised forest again and because of the midday sun, by the time they got there, they were quite wet under the arms and across the back.

The Captain was impressed by the doorway to the other dimension. "Although, is it meant to be like that—right-angled to each other? If I had a bit of time and my Train I could fix that. I suppose it doesn't really matter."

"It's just down this way a bit," said Laura.

"Tell you what," said the Captain, "is it just me, or does it feel, *different* being out of the Sanctuary?"

"I feel different," said Paulo, nodding. "A good different."

They walked a little further.

"I see that you're taking us to the Sanctuary Underground," said Mr. Cameron, "but why? I don't want to see this place again as long as I live."

"Are we going the right way?" Laura asked him.

"Yes I believe so, but . . ."

"Oh look, it's down there."

They followed her down an almost-concealed hole in the ground and found the concrete steps. As soon as they reached the bottom, Laura was racing around, evidently looking for something.

Paulo and the Captain were gob smacked by what they saw down there. It only made the Captain even more disgraced at what A1 had been trying to get away with.

"Here she is!!" they heard Laura calling from a little way away. Laura was crouching outside Evie's new little home. And even in that horrible place, Evie was in there jumping for joy.

"You scratch my back, I scratch yours," Laura said with a big smile and released Evie straight away. They hugged. And as soon as Evie saw Paulo, Mr. Cameron and the Captain approaching, she hugged each of them as well.

"Who are all these people?" Paulo said with shock.

"I assume they're all ex-residents of the Sanctuary," said the Captain, grimly. "People who didn't cooperate and were impossible to pin down. Am I right?"

Laura nodded. "Up in the Sanctuary, all these people have 'died'. A1 would make up some story. That's how I came to be down here. A1 finally trapped me—inescapably this time, put me in one of those teleport glass box things and I found myself down here. A1 should have realised I'd know he was bluffing when he said it was a disintegrator. What an idiot."

"I think that when you're at the end of your tether, you can start losing the plot and make mistakes," said the Captain. "You start becoming forgetful and careless—clutching at anything for a chance to get what you want."

"Well, hadn't we better release all these other people?" said Paulo.

"Not until we've found A1," said Mr. Cameron. "He must be down here somewhere."

They didn't have very far to walk.

"Ah ha, there you are," he said. There wasn't a hint of smugness. Mr. Cameron wasn't the sort to say 'Ha-ha, I told you so'.

A1 looked totally defeated, and slightly mad. He didn't fight to get out or try to say anything. He didn't even look up.

"What do we do from here?" asked Paulo.

"Well it's a shame to waste that beautiful place up there," said Mr. Cameron. "I was thinking of restoring it back to what it was first created for. A holiday resort. I could be the manager, and people can come from all over to have a restful, *temporary* holiday. How does that sound?"

"Sounds great!" said Laura.

"And I'll design that transportation service the council talked about in the beginning to get people to and from the planet. That'll be a project to keep me busy. I'll have to build up a good team of staff first. And there'll be no more playing 'follow the leader'. My staff will be working for me because they *want* to work for me. I don't suppose," he then said to the Captain and his crew, "would you like to stay on for a bit? A relaxing holiday?"

"I think not," said the Captain. "In fact, I'd like to be on my way. Right after we release all these people."

"Probably for the best. It'll take me a while to get it all re-developed and everything anyway. And don't worry about this," he said referring to all the poor people trapped in the glass prisons. "I'll get them all out and send them all home. All their records will be up in the Infirmary."

"What's going to happen to A1?" asked Evie.

"Who, old Geoffrey over there? I think I'll leave him down here until he's learnt his lesson. What do you reckon? Perhaps I'll get him slightly better quarters to stay in. And in a more convenient spot."

"What are *you* going to do, Laura?" Evie then said, with a hint of sadness in her eyes, knowing there would have to be a goodbye soon. "You don't want to come with us, do you? I'm sure the Captain would welcome you aboard."

"I'd love to, even though I don't even know where you're from, but um . . ." she started to look up at Mr. Cameron. "I was thinking of maybe staying on to help fix this place up, you know sort of, work for Mr. Cameron. If he'll have me of course."

"It's funny," said Ben Cameron. "I was just thinking I'd need an Assistant Manager. Welcome aboard." Then he whispered to the other three with a wink, "And I'll have to think about someone to continue the Sanctuary after I'm gone."

"This is going to be so totally cool! Ah, but first, can I just stay for a short holiday? But I want a luxury apartment. Not that pokey one I had before."

"Ha ha! Of course! You deserve it young lady!"

"And breakfast in bed every morning!"

"Oh, I'm not sure about that," he said tiredly.

"Well it sounds like an extremely happy ending for everybody," said the Captain, after they were back in the Sanctuary. They'd walked through the forest and were coming through to the square again. The sun was low. "Except . . . well, maybe A1 will get a happy ending eventually."

"I hope so," said Mr. Cameron.

"Look at this place," said the Captain. "It's eerie."

"It's morning here by the looks. The dimensions are slightly out of whack I believe."

"Everybody knows there's nothing doing. Everything is closed it's like a ruin. Everyone you see is half asleep. And we're on our own. We're in the street."

"Put your mind at rest, Captain," said the earnest Mr. Cameron. "I'll put it all right. Do you think you'll come and visit some time? For a holiday? Laura can serve the breakfast in bed."

"Possibly. But it won't be for a long time yet I don't think." The Captain shook Mr. Cameron's hand. Evie and Laura hugged tightly and said how glad they were to have met each other and thanked each other for their help. They all said a long farewell, but soon, the Captain was hustling them along, for he wasn't too good at goodbyes.

When they did eventually get back to that rocky beach, the sun was just rising. A brand new day in the Sanctuary.

"Evelyn, what you said astounded me," the Captain had said on their way back.

"What? Oh, when I was in the glass box? Well, I knew it wasn't really a disintegrator, *obviously*."

The Captain stopped walking and looked at her. "No you didn't. I saw the fear in your eyes."

"I thought you were amazing, Evie," added Paulo.

"Well I . . . just thought about all those people. I couldn't believe what I was saying, but I knew there was nothing else I could say. How could I plead for my life when that many others were at stake?"

"And now there are thousands of people who should be so grateful for what you did, but they'll never even know you."

Evie almost got caught up in the thought and felt rather flattered and special. But then she waved a hand, "Don't be silly. It was really Laura letting you know he was bluffing that saved the day."

"But you weren't to know that at the time. Come on, let's move."

"Fancy it being called *The Sanctuary*," Paulo said. "It kind of degrades that word a bit doesn't it."

The Captain agreed. "You know it's unbelievable what lengths people will go to to find a bit of rest."

"Well rest is a wonderful thing sometimes," said Paulo. "Isn't it worth it?"

"Yes but people are looking in the wrong places."

"Well *I* learnt something new about a sanctuary during that whole experience, you'll be glad to know," said Evie.

"What's that?"

"It isn't necessarily a place."

The Captain was getting the Train key out of one of his many pockets and as he inserted it in the lock, he said, taking one last glance at that beautiful, fresh, picturesque, peaceful place, "I shan't be at all sad to leave this place, how about you?"

"No way!" they said and hopped on board after the Captain.

"Now," the Captain said, reaching the Train's engine room, "I'm certain that after that experience, you surely couldn't not want to go home, Evelyn."

"I didn't even understand that. Too many double negatives. But it sounds like you're trying to get rid of me?"

"I'm not. But remember what I said when you first thought about travelling on the Train?"

"You said it was dangerous."

The Captain was serious for a moment, while he gave Evie some room to make another decision.

"Well," she said eventually, "Obviously I'm missing my mum and dad and my brother. And obviously I want to see them after watching them on that screen down in the Sanctuary Underground place . . . but . . . I reckon I could go on a bit longer. You know, to see a nebula from up in space again like we saw that first time, near Serothia. Or even to see a different species of animal—one that you wouldn't ever see on earth. A harmless one of course. On a harmless planet somewhere."

"You want to go on another trip?"

"Yes please," she replied straight away—hands behind her back, twisting from side to side and giving the Captain her sweetest smile.

"Alright. But we'll go to the most harmless place I can think of."

"Heaps good!"

"Sounds good to me, too!" said Paulo.

After the Captain set some coordinates (keeping it secret from the other two), he whirled into action and after that, the same could be said for the Train. The chugging sound came slowly first, as if it was warming up, and it gradually sped up little by little into that steady rhythmic steam-train sound:

__Chuff__ choofety chuff, choofety __chuff__ choofety bang!
Choofety __chuff__ choofety chuff, choofety __chuff__ choofety bang!
Choofety __chuff__ choofety chuff, choofety __chuff__ choofety bang!

It wasn't long until the Captain did something and the engine was slowing down again.

"Press that button there Evelyn," he said.

"What does it do?"

"It'll materialise us. We'll *enter space* again."

Evie could tell the Captain loved this whole travelling thing that he did. She pressed it and her stomach was buzzing with excitement. "Where are we?"

"You're free to explore," he said, pointing towards the door.

She smiled a nervous smile and then crept through the carriage room. When she got to the door with Paulo right behind her, she took a deep breath and blasted through.

The two of them stumbled out into the open air and Evie's face dropped dramatically.

"Captain!" she called over her shoulder. "That's not fair!"

The Captain was confused at her reaction.

"What is this place, Evie?" said Paulo. "You look as though you recognise it."

"I do. It's Adelaide. It's Earth. It's home!"

"What?" exclaimed the Captain and he came tumbling out of the Train too, bumping into the pair of them from behind. "That's odd."

"Don't pretend. I suppose you're right. I should let my parents know I'm okay, at least."

"No honestly," said the Captain. "That *wasn't* meant to happen! Believe me!" He paused and then frowned as he saw something cross the busy road that they were on the side of. "And I don't think *that's* supposed to happen either."

They all looked on. Both Evie and the Captain were utterly bemused and immediately frightened. Paulo wasn't so much, because on this planet, he didn't know what was normal and what wasn't.

But there it was, large as life, crossing the road at its own leisure.

A crocodile. A huge, green and gold, scaly, terrifying, real live crocodile.

Paulo was puzzled at Evie and the Captain's puzzled expressions. "I gather," he said, "that that animal doesn't typically wander the streets of Adelaide, then."

Then the crocodile spotted them, and started charging forward . . .

"*There is a time for everything, and a season for every activity under heaven.*"—*Ecclesiastes 3:1*

"*A false witness will not go unpunished, and he who pours out lies is ruined.*"—*Proverbs 19:9*

"*Rescue me and deliver me in your righteousness; turn your ear to me and save me. Be my rock of refuge, to which I can always go; give the command to save me, for you are my rock and my fortress.*"—*Psalm 71:2-3*

"*Rescue me from my enemies, O Lord, for I hide myself in you.*"—*Psalm 143:9*

"*You are my hiding place; you will protect me from trouble and surround me with songs of deliverance.*"—*Psalm 32:7*

"*It is better to take refuge in God than trust in people.*"—*Psalm 118:8*

"*Come to me (Jesus), all you who are weary and burdened and I will give you rest . . . I won't lay anything heavy or ill-fitting on you. Keep company with me and you'll learn to live freely and lightly.*"—*Matthew 11:28-30*

"*Blessed are you who give yourselves over to God, turn your backs on the world's 'sure thing', ignore what the world worships.*"—*Psalm 40:4*

"The Sanctuary" Facts

The Universe

The 'Swan Neck' Galaxy (or T47) is not a factual galaxy but an invention of mine.

The Captain's 'Beatles' Quotes

"Even Bungalow Bill took an elephant and a gun. And in case of accidents he always took his mum."

> from the song line "When out tiger hunting with his elephant and gun, in case of accidents he always took his mum."
> from the song: "The Continuing Story of Bungalow Bill"

"The boy with kaleidoscope eyes."

> from song line "A girl with kaleidoscope eyes"
> from the song "Lucy In The Sky With Diamonds"

"Everybody knows there's nothing doing. Everything is closed it's like a ruin. Everyone you see is half asleep. And we're on our own. We're in the street."

> from the line "Everybody knows there's nothing doing. Everything is closed it's like a ruin. Everyone you see is half asleep. And you're on your own. You're in the street."
> from the song "Good Morning"

Other

Nocturnal means active by night, so—an animal that comes out only at night and sleeps during the day. I made up the word Terafian though and there is no such thing (on Earth anyway) as a large Terafian short-tailed squirrel.